Her summer had j

A moose! Baby mooses! Was that the right word? Kerrie had never seen moose before in real life. They were magnificent! The dark brown mother so tall, her long stick-like legs seemingly incapable of bearing her great weight. The dark blonde youngsters, though lighter in color and smaller in scale, were perfect mirror images of their mother.

She turned to face an approaching vehicle, casting a last glance over her shoulder to make sure the moose cow and her calves did not reenter the road.

A large silver truck pulled up to the kiosk and Kerrie wished she could have slid down to the floor of her booth. The driver was Dace and he wore the same Smokey Bear hat as she, except as one of those outdoorsy men, it looked so much better on him. He worked for the Park Service. Her summer had just gotten much, much longer.

Kerrie's heart tapped an excited rhythm against her chest. If this was any indication of what the summer promised, her hiding place suddenly looked a lot like Paradise.

Bess McBride

A Trail of Love

by

Bess McBride

This is a work of fiction. Names, characters, places, and incidents are either the product of the author's imagination or are used fictitiously, and any resemblance to actual persons living or dead, business establishments, events, or locales, is entirely coincidental.

A Trail of Love

Contact Information: info@thewildrosepress.com

Cover Art by *Angela Anderson*

The Wild Rose Press
PO Box 706
Adams Basin, NY 14410-0706
Visit us at www.thewildrosepress.com

Publishing History
Last Rose Edition, 2008
PRINT ISBN 1-60154-299-2

Published in the United States of America

Dedication

For the hardworking people
at Glacier National Park...
and to Les for all your support.

Chapter One

Kerrie buried herself further into the overstuffed brocade easy chair and forced her eyes back to the pages of the book in her hands.

He stared at her again. She was sure of it. Of course, her imagination could be working overtime. After all, she wasn't *that* attractive. No one had ever said to her, "I fell in love with you the first time I saw you across the room." And that probably wasn't going to happen tonight either.

She eased out a small sigh, exquisitely aware of his scrutiny, both afraid and excited by his intent gaze, hoping he wouldn't see her discomfiture. Her traitorous eyes flicked in his direction. His dark head was bent, his attention firmly fixed on the book in his lap.

Kerrie, you twit, he's not even looking at you!

Her face reddened with the private embarrassment of her daydreams. She peeked at him again, hoping he wouldn't look up and catch her staring at him as she seemed compelled to do every time she saw him.

Was he kind? Could you tell if someone was gentle just by looking at them? She strained her neck to see the large hands holding the book in his lap. They looked strong, the fingers long and sturdy. He wore no rings. He held the book with care, turning the pages slowly and thoughtfully. If his hands were on her, would they touch her in just that way? Slowly, thoughtfully.

His long legs were crossed, the book resting on one bent blue-jeaned knee. *Long legs.* A source of concern. That meant he was tall. Her breathing quickened, turning shallow, and she forced herself to take a gulp of air. His only failing as far as she could see. He was tall.

Kerrie's eyes clouded as her thoughts traveled to the not too distant past for a few moments. When she willed herself back to the present, she found herself staring straight into a pair of warm gray eyes. With heated cheeks, she looked away quickly, but not before she saw a charming smile light up his face. She buried her head in her book again and made a valiantly nonchalant effort to shift in her large seat...away from him.

Stop it, she cursed herself. He wasn't the one. There wasn't going to be one. Ever. He'd only smiled because he caught her ogling him. Anyone could smile. That didn't make them safe.

Her heart pounded in her throat and she dragged in another deep breath to help slow it down. She didn't know why it raced. Fear, excitement, nerves. It didn't matter. She didn't want her heart to beat fast anymore. She just wanted a comfortable, boring life where her toughest decision concerned whether to eat cream of tomato soup or cream of potato soup for dinner.

"Excuse me, I think you dropped this," a deep resonant voice spoke from above her head.

She started and her eyes flew up to find him standing over her, holding her cell phone. She stared at the phone in confusion. It was definitely hers, the battered dents and dings unmistakably marked it as her often-dropped phone.

He held out the phone, a wide relaxed grin on his face.

"I saw it on the floor, and I didn't want you to leave without it."

A familiar shaking began in her hands and spread throughout her body. Please don't stand over me, she pleaded silently. She couldn't jump up from the chair because his close proximity blocked her exit. She would look foolish if she suddenly vaulted over the overstuffed arm of the chair, but she was on the verge of doing just that.

With lowered eyes, she reached a trembling hand to take the phone. He backed up slightly. Kerrie grabbed the phone and ungracefully rose and extricated herself from the tight situation.

"Thank you," she mumbled, her eyes lowered to the phone grasped tightly in her hand.

"You're welcome. My name is Dace, by the way." He held out a large, capable hand. The rules of a proper upbringing forced her to put her small, cold shaking hand in his. She felt certain he jumped at the ice cube she put in his hand.

"Kerrie" she said shortly as she waited for him to pull his hand away from her frigid one. He didn't though, and the steady warmth of his hand began to course throughout her frozen body.

She pulled her hand away and put it behind her back.

"Well, thank you again," she dismissed him, hoping he would go away. She couldn't bear to have him so near. Her body betrayed her with its trembling and weakness, her hard-won strength deserted her. Barely suppressed anxiety rose to choke the oxygen from her lungs.

"It was nice meeting you. I've got to run," Kerrie mumbled as she bent down to grab her bag from the floor beside the chair and stuff her cell phone into it. She left the book on the chair, too frazzled to reshelve it as was her practice. She had been thinking about buying it, but obviously not at the moment. No time to think.

"Wait. Your book," he called out to her retreating back. She heard him but kept going, hoping to get lost in the aisles of books as she made her way out of the busy store and into the late afternoon sun. She threw herself in her small truck with a sigh of relief. No time to celebrate her escape though. What if he followed her to tell her she had left the book behind?

She put the car into gear and flew out of the parking lot, keeping her eyes straight ahead. A quick glance in her rearview mirror revealed he had exited the building, but he seemed intent on heading to his own vehicle and did not glance in her direction. Nevertheless, on her drive home, Kerrie kept her eyes in her rearview mirror, checking frequently to see if she was being followed.

She urged herself to stop making such a fuss about everything. The man simply returned her dropped phone. He wasn't stalking her. He did not have a crush on her and he wasn't madly in love with her. He was simply a stranger in a bookstore whom she saw occasionally, who both frightened and attracted her. She'd do best to forget him. He was trouble. Weren't they all?

She reached her small apartment in one piece and stepped inside the small one-bedroom sanctuary. She dropped her bag on a side table and crossed to the windows to survey the view. She'd been so lucky to find this little treasure. The snow-capped mountains in the distance provided a magnificent backdrop to a nearby large meadow where horses grazed and frisked. The occasional deer popped in to graze alongside his domesticated four-legged friends.

Her cell phone rang, and she studied the caller identification before she answered it. Always. Her mother. The underlying current of anxiety which continued to course through her body lessened as she heard her mother's loving voice.

"Hi, Mom."

"Hi, honey. How are you?"

"Good," she lied.

"Really?" questioned her skeptical mother. "You sound a little winded."

Kerrie sighed. She could never hide anything from her mother, but she wanted her parents to believe that she was getting better. *She* wanted to believe that she was getting better.

"I'm okay, Mom," she said with resignation. "I'm still getting a little anxious, that's all. Especially around strangers." She told her mother about the encounter with the stranger in the bookstore and her subsequent reaction. She left out the fact that she indulged in the occasional romantic fantasy with him as the star.

"Oh, honey, I'm so sorry. I wish you could be here with us. You're so far away." Her mother's voice held a promise of safety and security, warmth and companionship, but experience had shown that it was an illusion.

You can't go back home again.

She couldn't ever be a child again. The world would not go away.

"I know, Mom. I wish I could too," she lied once more. Well, maybe not completely. "But I'm nested in here now, and it's a fine little town. I'm enjoying myself."

"Well, you probably don't need to get involved with any men yet anyway. Have you made any female friends?"

"No, not yet. I will, Mom, I will," she pacified her worried parent. She really had no intention of making any friends. Acquaintances were all she could handle, the cashier at the corner grocery store, the manager of the apartment building, the barista at the local java joint. That would be the extent of her new world.

"Your dad's out golfing today or I'd put him on the phone."

"That's okay, Mom. I'm not feeling real chatty anyway. How's his health?"

She heard a low chuckle on the other end of the line. "Oh, you know Dad, Kerrie. He'll live to be 100."

"And how are you, Mom?"

"I'm fine, honey. I miss you, that's all. I wish we could come see you to see if you're settled in okay." She heard the wistfulness in her mother's voice, and she wished her life was different. Why couldn't she live near her home where her parents would be nearby? She could eat dinner with them on Sunday, shop with her mother, and drive the golf cart for her father. Why couldn't she?

Tears threatened to choke her voice as she replied, "I'm really okay, Mom. I don't think you guys should come here...not yet anyway. I need to be alone for a while."

"I know, honey. That was the plan. It just breaks my heart to think of you alone."

"Everything's okay, Mom. I'm actually enjoying it," she did her best to cheer her mother up. "I'm content."

"Content," her mother echoed bitterly. There was an unanswered pause and then her mother lightened her tone. "Good, I'm glad to hear it. I'm going to start making dinner. Dad should be home soon. Call me tomorrow, okay?"

"Okay, Mom. Good night. Say hi to Dad for me. And give Suzie a kiss for me." She chuckled anticipating her mother's reaction.

"I will give your father a kiss for you, but I will not kiss the dog. However, she misses you, and I'll tell her you called. She sits on Dad's lap every night now. I'm not sure he's going to want to give her up when you're ready to take her."

Kerrie was hopeful. "Good, let him keep her. I miss her terribly, but I can't take care of her right now. I'm not home enough."

"Okay, hon, we'll take of her. I love you. Good night."

"Night, Mom."

Kerrie hung up the phone and stared at the mountains through the window. Suzie would have loved to romp in the meadow below, but Kerrie doubted the horses would have appreciated the little varmint. She missed the little poodle mix she'd adopted from the animal shelter two years ago. Maybe someday she'd find another dog like her. Someday.

****

Kerrie donned her Smokey Bear hat early the next morning and studied herself critically in the mirror of her small bathroom. She looked silly in the broad-brimmed hat, she was sure of it. It didn't flatter everybody, just bears, handsome outdoorsy men, and tall, athletic young blonde women. Kerrie was a short brunette with hair too thick and curly to accommodate the hat properly. It didn't matter. She had to wear the hat anyway. It was part of the job.

She stepped out of her apartment and into the brisk cool air of early summer in the Rocky Mountains of Montana. She couldn't believe she still needed her jacket in May, but this was high country, and the nights would be cool throughout the summer.

I should have headed for Florida, she mumbled silently as she made her way to the small blue truck in front of the apartment building. A tiny chipmunk sitting on a small boulder near her parking spot chattered away.

"Good morning, Chipper. How are you?" Kerrie smiled for the first time that day. She relaxed and leaned against the truck for a moment watching the little fellow with the big eyes and racing stripes down his back alternately chatter and nibble at some small morsel of food.

"Well, I'd like to stay and chat, but I've got to get to work. I've got a twenty minute drive ahead of me. Be good and I'll see you when I get home, okay?" She wished she had some food to give him, but the little guy looked well fed. Besides, she didn't want to come out tomorrow morning and find twenty chipmunks sitting on her truck waiting for breakfast.

With a lingering smile on her face, Kerrie jumped in, backed out of the parking lot, and headed toward the highway. She turned off her radio, preferring to listen to the sound of wind blowing in the trees, birds of prey screeching overhead, or perhaps the bugle of an elk. She rolled down her window and reveled in the beauty of the lush green valley as she headed toward the mountains.

Her unruly thoughts soon turned to the man in the bookstore. She wondered if he would be there again that evening. She'd fallen into the habit of going into the bookstore/coffee shop combo every night for a cup of hot chocolate and a few pages of a good book. With too much solitary time on her hands, she'd already bought enough romance novels to fill a bookcase in the few short weeks she'd been in Montana.

Buying books and drinking hot chocolate helped pass the time. She couldn't hold back a sly grin. Chocolate and romance! Was there ever a combination more suited to feeling good? Relatively harmless habits, they helped warm her spirits on the cold and lonely nights in a strange, new town.

Kerrie slowed to round a bend in the canyon towering above the Middle Fork of the Flathead River. The milky blue-green water still ran high from spring runoff. Three white-tail deer stood on the opposite bank grazing, their coats russet red against the emerald green of the trees along the river.

Kerrie had seen Dace in the bookstore a few times before. His handsome looks caught her eye...but, as her mother noted on the phone the night before, she really didn't need to be ogling men right now. In fact, that was the last thing she should be doing. She needed to learn to be on her own.

An unbidden image of Dace standing over her came to mind, and she couldn't suppress the shudder that passed through her. As handsome as he was, he was still tall, and she had no intention of getting involved with anyone bigger than her in the future. In fact, she had no intention of getting involved with anyone. Period!

She entered the Park at the West Entrance and pulled into the parking lot. Only her second week on the job, she continued to be nervous and unsure of herself. She attempted to strike a confident pose, but found it a bit disconcerting with the huge Smokey Bear style hat perched on her dark curls. She pushed a hand up to adjust it and opened the door of the office.

Sandy, one of those statuesque athletic blonde women Kerrie thought of earlier, had arrived early and made herself a cup of coffee. Her taupe and forest green uniform fit her six foot frame like a glove, and *her* ranger hat gave her an air of authority which Kerrie could only admire.

"Morning, Kerrie. How are you today?"

"Good. How are you?"

"Tired. 6 o'clock came early this morning. You must be getting up earlier than I am if you're living in Columbia Falls. That's a bit of a drive, isn't it? It's too bad park housing was full when you got here."

"Oh, that's okay. It's a nice drive. I have a quiet apartment. I'm not sure how I'd feel living in the dormitories here." She shook her head when Sandy offered her a cup of coffee. Not without mocha. Sometimes, she missed the convenience of the big city, the java joints on every corner.

"I don't blame you. This stuff is rotgut. I just have to have one cup in the morning to get going." Sandy wrapped her hands around her steaming mug and grinned an orthodontured bright smile.

Kerrie returned the hard-to-resist smile of the friendly woman. Sandy had been doing seasonal work in the parks for about five years, and Kerrie looked up to the tall woman—literally—for her expertise though Sandy was in her mid-twenties and Kerrie just turned forty.

"How are you enjoying the job so far? It's fun, isn't it? Wait till we really get going in July and August. It'll be nonstop visitors," Sandy raised her beautiful light brown eyebrows in an exaggerated wag. "I love it."

"I'm having fun so far," Kerrie responded to Sandy's infectious enthusiasm. "I wish I knew what I was doing, but that will come in time, I guess."

"Every park is different. This is my fourth park in five years. I was here last year. So, just as soon as you figure out how this park works, you might be on to another one, and the job will be completely different." Sandy looked down at her watch. "Seven o'clock. Time for us to open the kiosk, I guess."

"I think I'm on the gate this morning. This is my first

shift by myself. Wish me luck!"

Sandy pulled open the door and handed Kerrie her cash drawer. "Piece of cake," she murmured. "It's early in the season yet."

Kerrie walked over to the kiosk, only ten feet away from the office, and met Sam, her supervisor, who unlocked the kiosk.

"Morning, Kerrie. Are you nervous about your first day alone out here?" The short, stout, bald-headed lead supervisor smiled. Even his ranger hat looked good on him. In fact, he looked a bit like a Marine drill instructor, which he had been in a previous life.

She nodded. No point in lying. Maybe he would stay with her all day.

"You'll be fine," he said in a firm voice. "Your hat's crooked." Kerrie's cheeks burned as he reached over to straighten her hat with all the experience of a drill sergeant instructing new recruits. She reached up a tentative hand to check the balance after he straightened it.

"Sorry, it's my hair. It's out of control." She made a rueful face.

"Mine too," he grinned unexpectedly.

She laughed at his unexpected humor. The laugh felt good. Up to now, he'd been fairly professional, if not a bit dour, but his sharp blue eyes continued to twinkle as he dropped his smile and squared his chin.

"If you have any questions, call me or Sandy over in the office on the intercom. Sandy will be out in an hour and a half to relieve you. I've got to take off and run back to headquarters. Are you set?" he asked, the twinkle in his eye continuing to dance.

"I'm set," she replied with a grin. The corner of his mouth twitched, but didn't break a smile. He saluted her with two fingers to the brim of his hat, headed off to a waiting park vehicle, and drove off.

Alone, on the gate. *Oh, please, don't let anyone come yet. I don't know what to do.*

It didn't seem to matter what Kerrie wanted because a small station wagon barreled down the road toward the gate. She pulled herself together, and as she had seen and practiced during training, she leaned out the window and said to the elderly couple in the car, "Welcome to Glacier National Park." She quoted the entrance fee and gave them their receipt, a park map, and a brochure. A successful transaction completed with no disaster, she happily waved goodbye to the cheerful couple and sat back down on her stool.

She had just perched on the edge of her seat when she saw a moose and two calves step out of the trees and enter the roadway 100 yards in front of the kiosk. She held her breath, hoping a car would not hurtle down the road while the slow moving creature regally proceeded across. The large cow turned a watchful eye toward the shack, but dismissed Kerrie as any danger. She continued amiably across the road until she reached the grass on the other side. With a leap over a small gully, she disappeared into the trees. Her ungainly calves followed in a splay of legs.

A moose! Baby mooses! Was that the right word? Kerrie had never seen moose before in real life. They were magnificent! The dark brown mother so tall, her long stick-like legs seemingly incapable of bearing her great weight. The dark blonde youngsters, though lighter in color and smaller in scale, were perfect mirror images of their mother.

Kerrie's heart tapped an excited rhythm against her chest. If this was any indication of what the summer promised, her hiding place suddenly looked a lot like Paradise.

She turned to face an approaching vehicle, casting a last glance over her shoulder to make sure the moose cow and her calves did not reenter the road.

A large silver truck pulled up to the kiosk and Kerrie wished she could have slid down to the floor of her booth. The driver was Dace and he wore the same Smokey Bear hat as she, except as one of those outdoorsy men, it looked so much better on him. He worked for the Park Service. Her summer had just gotten much, much longer.

Chapter Two

"Well, I wondered where you worked," Dace said with a wide grin. He cast a quick glance in his rearview mirror and turned his engine off.

Kerrie's eyes widened. Was he planning on staying to chat for a while? This time, she had no escape.

"I knew you worked for the Park Service, but no one seemed to know who you were," he added. "I asked around," he grinned broadly. "Is this your first day on the gate?"

Kerrie nodded mutely. He'd asked about her? She rummaged through her brain for some witty comment.

"Yes, my first day," she replied cleverly.

"How's it going so far?" Friendly blue-gray eyes framed by dark lashes studied her. His even-toothed smile brought out weathered crinkles at the corners of his eyes.

Kerrie would have given anything to shut the window of the kiosk and disappear from sight, but some small measure of reality retained its grip on her, and she knew that was impossible.

"Good," she replied briefly. "Is that a car coming?" She made a pretense of peering down the road.

From the corner of her eye, she saw him check his rearview mirror and then grin.

"No, I've got time."

He held out his hand. "Dace Mitchell," he said. "I didn't get a chance to introduce myself last night. I'm a ranger here."

Reluctantly, she reached out to shake his hand. He grasped hers lightly, and fortunately for her, he let it go quickly. She thought she would panic if he had given her one of those firm, long-lasting handshakes some people were wont to do.

"Kerrie Gowen," she replied, pointing to her nametag. She glanced down the road, relieved to see a real vehicle approaching at last.

Dace saw it as well and turned on his engine. "Looks like I'd better get out of the way. It was nice to meet you, Kerrie Gowen. I'll see you again. Have a good day." He gave her one of those devastating grins as he waved and pulled away.

A quick mental lecture served to remind Kerrie not to fall for his easy charm. She had no idea what the man was like. A warm smile could hide anything. Smiles did not guarantee safety.

The approaching car pulled up and she fended off thoughts of a painful past by busying herself with the visitors.

****

Kerrie arrived home late in the afternoon and debated on going to the bookstore. She longed to go, but what if Dace showed up? What if he didn't? Conflicted about him and about her choices, a restless energy would not allow her to settle down at home with a good book. The night stretched endlessly, and in her isolation, she feared she might fall off the face of the earth with no one to know.

She grabbed a quick sandwich, promising herself that if Dace showed up in the bookstore, she would leave before he saw her. It was possible he wouldn't appear at any rate. She'd only seen him there a couple times. He did not attend as compulsively as she. He probably doesn't have my hot chocolate addiction, she thought whimsically. Didn't know what he was missing.

Kerrie pulled up to the unexpectedly large bookstore and made her way through the oversize wooden doors. With a grimace of frustration, she found herself ducking her head and lowering her eyes...like some sort of fugitive. The term seemed particularly apt at times. In fact, she supposed the description fit her quite well.

She grumbled silently. One of the satisfactions of being an anonymous stranger in a small town was that she shouldn't know anyone well enough to have to hide from them. She hadn't been here a month and already she hid from a man. She narrowed her eyes, raised her chin defiantly, and asserted that she would not hide from anyone in the bookstore. It was a free country. If Dace was there, so be it. His presence had nothing to do with her and would not affect her in the least.

"May I help you?" the young barista asked with a smile. Kerrie remembered the day when she knew all the baristas at her favorite city coffee shop. But in this small town, she continued to hold back, to maintain her reserve—ever the stranger.

"Could I have a large hot chocolate, please?" she asked, willing herself not to look around. She just wanted peace.

"No whip cream, right?" the friendly brunette teenager asked.

"No, thanks," Kerrie smiled.

"I've got it memorized. I'll have it right up." Deenie, as her nametag read, busied herself with steaming milk while Kerrie struggled not to gawk at her fellow booklovers.

A tall bearded man in a flannel shirt and jeans approached the coffee bar, coming to rest beside her. With an uncontrollable shiver, Kerrie moved a foot away. Aware of what she had done and hoping he wouldn't notice, she stole a peek up at his face. He looked down at her with a cursory glance before he turned his head to the woman who came up behind him.

"Did you order my drink, hon?" the woman asked.

"Not yet. Waiting in line," he replied.

Kerrie's face flushed. She hoped no one noticed her maneuver.

Deenie handed her a tall steaming cup of hot chocolate. "Here you are," she said with a flourish before turning to the next customer.

Kerrie took her drink and headed to the seating area, already warming to the prospect of burrowing into a comfortable chair while she relished her hot drink.

Due to the early hour just before dinner, the store seemed fairly empty. Only a few other booklovers lounged about, perusing magazines and novels. A quick survey revealed Dace was not among them.

Kerrie gratefully found a chair and dropped into it. She quickly realized she'd forgotten to get something to read, but before she jumped up again, she took a long slow sip of her drink and thoughtfully studied the people in the store. Ordinary people. One would never know they lived in a small Montana town. They didn't necessarily sport cowboy boots or hats, smell of cow manure or sheep, have weathered skin or narrow slit eyes from scanning the prairies. In fact, several customers sported casual gym clothes and sneakers while others wore miniskirts and kitten heels. She could just as easily have been sitting in a large chain bookstore in a major West Coast city.

Kerrie wasn't sure what to expect when she came to this small town. Certainly safety and security, the primary driving forces behind her escape. Anonymity. Peace, serenity. A new beginning.

She shook her head slightly to dispel encroaching memories and rose in search of an entertaining book, leaving her drink on the table beside her chair. She headed to her favorite travel section and stopped in front of the books on Montana. She'd read many of the books and had purchased quite a few, but never tired of the subject. She reached for a coffee table book of scenic photographs when she heard a voice to her right.

"Hello again, Kerrie. How was your first day on the gate?"

Kerrie swung her head to the right and found herself standing less than a foot away from a very tall Dace who regarded her with a bright grin on his tanned face. Startled by his close proximity, she backed up quickly and stumbled over a stepstool in the aisle.

"Whoa." Dace reached out with both arms to grab her as she fell against the bookshelves. He caught her before she fell to the floor and pulled her to her feet like a rag doll. She almost fell into his arms.

Kerrie knew he was only trying to help, but instinct kicked in and she pulled out of his grasp with a twist and an involuntary shudder. A flush heated her cheeks when she recovered enough to catch her breath and look at him to apologize. Dark gray eyes stared hard at her. A twitching muscle in his jaw gave evidence of his thoughts.

He held his hands up. "Look, Kerrie, I was only trying to keep you from falling. Don't get any ideas. I wasn't making a pass at you."

"I'm not," she responded hotly. "I'm not getting any ideas," she sputtered. "I'm sure you weren't," she said. Her eyes flitted from one side of the aisle to the other in a subconscious search for escape.

Dace stepped back to let her pass. “Please, don’t let me keep you,” he said with an edge. “You look like a trapped animal. I certainly didn’t mean to bother you.”

“You didn’t, I’m sorry,” she whispered as she hurried past him and flew out of the store. She jumped into her truck and drove away, uncertain of where she was headed.

How humiliating...and stupid. That was the first time she’d been close to a man since she’d run from Jack. Aghast at her behavior, she realized her visceral reaction to his grasp had been involuntary. She could not have behaved any other way, she was certain of that.

But he could have been a bit more understanding, couldn’t he? She wrung her hands on the wheel, knowing the answer. Of course not. She’d treated him like he had a contagious disease.

She drove on through the night, heading home, her hot chocolate growing cold on a table in the bookstore. She wasn’t sure she would ever be able to go there again. The serenity of the comforting easy chair and companionable books seemed lost.

****

Dace saw her cup sitting on the table, her name written on the outside by the barista. He lowered himself into the seat and picked up the cup. It was still hot. She hadn’t been here long, he thought. She flew out of the store, and he assumed she wasn’t coming back.

He set his jaw as he studied the cup. Why had she taken off like that? Maybe she didn’t like him. Maybe she didn’t like men in general. He’d never seen her with a man. He shook his head impatiently. That didn’t mean anything. She was here for seasonal summer work. She might have left someone behind.

He set the cup back down on the table. Shame coursed through his body. He’d been rude to her. It wasn’t like him to be sarcastic. He wasn’t sure why he’d reacted that way when she pulled away from him. Embarrassment maybe. But he hadn’t been making a pass at her. Really. He only wanted to help her when she tripped...because he’d startled her. That’s it, he thought. She was scared, not mad. She seemed to be afraid of him.

He unwound his long legs and rose slowly, staring at the lonely cup on the table. He considered himself a fairly harmless man. What had he done to frighten her? He shook his head slightly as he wandered slowly out of the bookstore with his hands stuffed in his denim pockets. The place just didn't seem the same without her there. He'd lost interest in reading anything that night.

He drove slowly out of the parking lot, wondering how to approach the skittish woman. How could he make it up to her? From the first time he'd seen her across the room...

Dace shook his head with a rueful grin.

Slow down, man. Life isn't a fairytale.

****

Kerrie stayed in the office the following morning, stuffing brochures, sorting through visitors guides. As much as she enjoyed working the gate the day before, she didn't want to be stuck there if Dace came through.

"Morning, Kerrie," said Sam as he entered the office. He removed his ranger hat and reverently placed it on a high shelf out of harms' way. "Do you have everything you need?" he asked briskly, casting a critical eye at the office supplies.

She smiled widely at her supervisor, more at ease with him now that she was aware a generous sense of humor lay beneath his brisk and professional exterior.

"Good morning, Sam. Yes, I'm fine," she said, looking around. "No questions so far." She reached a hand up to check the angle of her hat.

"It's straight," he said without smiling. "I already checked." The twinkle was back in his blue eyes.

Kerrie's cheeks felt warm, but she grinned through her embarrassment. "Thanks," she murmured, trying to keep her head straight.

"You look tired," Sam observed, looking down at his watch. She had the early shift this morning.

"Really? I didn't realize," Kerrie mumbled. "I don't think I slept well last night."

She was hoping he would take her statement at face value. He crossed his arms and leaned against the counter.

"Why not?" he asked abruptly.

"Oh, uh, I'm not sure." She had no intention of describing the long restless night of dreams...with Dace's face taking a prominent position. "Just one of those nights, I guess. You know."

"Not really," he said. "I sleep like a log. At least, that's what my wife says."

Kerrie remembered the small athletic-looking woman she'd met during newcomer orientation. "How is Mary?" she asked, finding a good opening to deflect the conversation away from her.

"Good. She's knee-deep in training some new seasonal park rangers." If Sam had a soft spot, his adventurous, outdoorsy hiking wife was it. A small smile warmed his lips.

"How many parks have you two worked?" Kerrie asked curiously.

"Geez, a bunch. We've been here about four years now, but before that, we were at Rocky Mountain National Park. Spent a few years at Yellowstone, a couple at Yosemite. Even did a couple years at Great Smokey Mountain National Park. Mary really loved it there, but we decided to move on. Lots of country to see."

Kerrie was as much taken aback at the unusual length of his speech as she was by how much they had traveled.

"Wow, you guys have been to a bunch of different places," she said appreciatively.

"Yeah, we enjoy traveling. Did it in the Marine Corps and found we couldn't stop when I retired. Mary especially. She was so used to packing up the house every three years while I was in the Corps that she gets antsy when we stay too long in one place. Suits me," he shrugged. "How about you? This is your first year with the National Park Service, isn't it?"

Kerrie nodded. "I've never traveled any further than from Spokane to here. My family's been in Western Washington forever. They've always stayed in one place. They never really traveled much either. Homebodies. My mother is quite worried about my being *so far from home*." Kerrie blushed. It sounded silly. She was almost 40 years old.

Sam raised his brows and gave her an awkward grin.

"Well, welcome to the Park Service. I think you'll enjoy seeing new places. I hope you do anyway." He looked at his watch again. "Well, I'd better get out and check on James and see he's doing. Then I've got to run and get supplies. I'll see you in a few hours."

"Bye, Sam." Kerrie waved as he strode out the door. She replayed the conversation with Sam over in her mind. Listening to herself talk, she realized how small her world had been, perhaps still was. She felt inadequate somehow, reporting that she'd never traveled before. Not that Sam had said anything to make her feel bad, but the realization that there were people who followed adventure, who dared enough to pursue the unknown and chase their dreams, made her wonder what she'd been doing with her life until now. Had it been a life well lived?

The hour passed quickly and it was soon time to replace James on the gate. Kerrie grabbed her cash drawer, adjusted her hat for the hundredth time, and strode over to the kiosk.

"Was it busy when you got here this morning?" the tall, lanky youth asked.

"No, not really. I guess it gets busier later on in the season, huh?"

"Yeah, this is my second year here. Last year, it was pretty slow this early in the year. Going to the Sun Road is still closed by snow, and that's what most people want to see." He pushed his glasses back and grinned at her. "How are you enjoying it so far?"

She looked up at him and returned his smile. She hadn't missed the fact that he was tall, but so far that had not been a problem. She had kept a safe co-worker distance from him. He stood outside the kiosk now, holding his cash drawer, having swapped places with her. He seemed harmless.

"It's great. I'm having a good time."

"Hey, did I see you talking to Dace Mitchell yesterday morning at the gate?" He explained. "I was walking over from the housing area."

Kerrie stiffened. "Oh yes, Dace. I just met him. Park ranger."

"Yeah. He was here last year. He's a permanent employee. Man, that's who I want to be when I grow up," he said reverently as he leaned against the kiosk, seemingly in no hurry to leave.

Kerrie scanned the empty road ahead and returned her gaze to James' worshiping face.

"Why?"

"It's hard to explain. Ever since I was a little kid, I wanted to be a park ranger. My parents took me to Yellowstone when I was a kid, and I got the bug. The outdoors, the animals, this cool uniform." He pulled himself up and squared his shoulders.

Kerrie couldn't help but grin. She had to admit the uniform looked quite smart on him.

"Well, I must say, you do wear the uniform well, James," she said with a chuckle. She was touched to see his cheeks stain red.

"Yeah, but not like Dace. He's the kind of park ranger I'd like to be. That guy is so cool. Did you know that last year, he led a police unit into the mountains to track down two kidnappers? One of them got away from the police and Dace chased him down and tackled him. They found the girl that had been kidnapped. Then I heard that three years ago, when he was at Yellowstone, he was attacked by a grizzly sow. He managed to get away without having to shoot her. I hear he's got the scars to prove it."

Kerrie's eyes widened. Scars on that handsome body. She couldn't bear the thought.

"I didn't know all that. My goodness, he is "Ranger Rick," isn't he?"

James grinned. "Yeah, he is. He's had a lot of adventures according to the rumor mill. He doesn't talk about them much though. Not one to blow his horn."

A car pulled up to the kiosk and Kerrie turned her attention to the visitors, hoping that James would remain to gossip. It seemed there was more to learn about Dace.

"Well, I'd better get in and count my drawer so I can go on break," James murmured to her back.

Kerrie waved at the departing tourists and turned to watched James' retreating back with disappointment. She found herself suffering from a mild case of hero worship herself, and she wanted to know more about the man who fought bears and kidnappers.

"Good morning, Kerrie."

With a gasp, Kerrie swung around to face the man who stood at the window on the other side of the kiosk.

Chapter Three

Kerrie jumped away from the window. Her survival instinct robbed her of all common sense. She stared wildly at Dace, heart pounding in her throat and choking her voice. Dace took a step back, and Kerrie watched the grin from his face disappear.

"Kerrie?"

"Dace," she choked out. "Oh, Hi." She struggled against her initial panic.

"Did I scare you?" Dace kept his distance. He narrowed his eyes and tilted his head inquiringly.

"Yes, I... Wow! I jumped. Sorry about that." Kerrie did her best to play off the visceral fear that gripped her only moments before.

"I'm sorry. I shouldn't have startled you." He shook his head and rubbed the back of his neck. Kerrie did her best to affect a nonchalant pose when he returned his blue-gray gaze to her face.

"Oh, don't worry about it. I'm just jumpy I guess."

He studied her face for an excruciating moment before speaking. "Well, listen, I was wondering if you've seen Sandy. I stopped by the office to ask James, but he hasn't seen her."

"Sandy." Kerrie repeated the name, her heart plummeting to her feet.

"Yeah, we're supposed to meet for lunch. She's always late though." The quick white grin Dace flashed did nothing to ease the turmoil his words created in Kerrie's poor addled brain.

Dace and Sandy were a couple. How foolish she had been—drooling over him at the bookstore, fantasizing about him in her dreams, placing him on a pedestal of heroic proportions.

Just then, her eye caught a movement in the parking lot. Sandy arrived in a government vehicle, apparently having run some official errands.

Without a word, Kerrie pointed to Sandy emerging from the small SUV.

Dace followed her hand.

"There she is. Thanks, Kerrie." He turned away, but stopped and turned back toward her. He dipped his head to peer into her veiled eyes. "I'm sorry I startled you. I'll see you soon. Okay?"

Kerrie clamped her mouth shut and nodded.

She watched Dace head over to speak to Sandy at her car and then she turned away. Luckily, a car pulled up to distract her. When the car passed through, she reluctantly turned back to survey the parking lot in time to see Dace drive off in his patrol vehicle with Sandy perched in the passenger seat.

Kerrie plopped down on her stool, shaking her head as she watched the retreating ranger SUV. What a fool she'd been—Sandy and Dace. Of course! And why not? She was tall and beautiful. He was tall and equally...beautiful.

Kerrie struggled to take a deep breath, though it seemed certain an elephant sat on her chest. Disappointment gave her body a heaviness that threatened to make it impossible to rise from the stool any time soon.

He wasn't available. Not that she cared, of course, but... What did she expect? That someone special was waiting for her to come along? This was the worst time in her life to be ogling a man. Hadn't she just escaped an impossible situation? And weren't tall men to be avoided?

She shook her head impatiently and forced herself to pay attention to the oncoming cars.

****

Kerrie took herself off to the bookstore that evening with a forced defiance. After all, Dace was dating someone, so she no longer needed to pine over him or feel ill at ease in his presence. He could come in and out of the bookstore all he wanted, she thought. It wouldn't bother her in the least. Maybe Sandy would come with him one night and they could all sit down and have a chat. Maybe they could get together for pinochle, she thought with a hysterical giggle.

Kerrie held her head high as she ordered her drink

and posted herself in her favorite easy chair. She remembered to grab a book on the way, and she buried her head in it, barely lifting her eyes to locate her cup as she forced her attention on the book with a fierce determination to enjoy herself.

An hour passed and Dace did not appear. Kerrie began to relax as it seemed clear that he would not come to the bookstore that evening, not an unusual circumstance. His appearances did not smack of the same ritualism as her visits. Kerrie often railed against the constricting routines she created for herself, but she'd never known any other way of living. Her childhood had consisted of breakfast, school, dinner, TV, and bedtime...week after week. Summers had been a bit less predictable, the occasional backyard barbecue, a small plastic swimming pool and endless hours of splashing, an annual vacation to her grandparent's farm a hundred miles away. Life had been simple, uncomplicated, carefree.

She stared unfocused when Dace walked into her view. Kerrie stiffened when she saw him and quickly dropped her eyes to the book lying open in her lap to assume her uninterruptible preoccupation with reading. From under veiled lashes, she saw his long legs approach. She gritted her teeth and started chanting silently.

Everything would be fine. The man had a girlfriend. He was just being nice. She should return his pleasantries. There was no excuse for rudeness.

Dace put a large hot drink down on the table next to her.

"May I sit here?" he asked, indicating the chair next to hers.

She looked up into his tanned face, noting with a catch in her breath how brilliantly his gray eyes shone.

"Sure," she indicated in her best careless tone.

"This is for you," Dace gestured toward the drink as he sank down into his chair. Though the chairs engulfed her short frame, he looked quite comfortable in his.

"Me?" Kerrie squeaked, studying the drink labeled hot chocolate. "What for?"

He grinned. "Because you didn't get to finish your drink last night. I was tempted to deliver it to you, but I don't know where you live. Seemed a shame to waste it."

"I...uh...oh, I'd forgotten I'd left it sitting on the table." She gave the table an accusing stare...anything to avoid looking at Dace. "You didn't have to," she finished lamely.

"I wanted to," he said firmly. With another quick grin, he opened the book in his hand and began to read.

Kerrie was nonplussed. So, he didn't intend to talk to her. Well, then why did he sit next to her? There were other chairs in the reading room.

In the ensuing silence, Kerrie fidgeted and gave herself a mental lecture. Dace was not interested in her...in *that* way. He was just in the bookstore to read a book. That was all. She needed to stop trying to read more into his presence than there was. And how could she forget Sandy? Who could tear their eyes away from her golden beauty?

Hyper alert to his close proximity, she only managed to scan the same lines repeatedly in her book. She turned pages occasionally to make it look...or sound...like she was reading, but she had no idea what the book was even about. She stole an occasional glance at Dace from under her lashes, but he seemed involved with his book.

She reached a tentative hand out for the drink he'd bought her. He would think she was being rude if she didn't drink it. She took a sip of the hot drink, ignoring her original drink now growing cold. She swallowed the sweet liquid in a euphoric flush of sensory delight. It had to be the best hot chocolate they had ever made. So smooth, silky, and rich in taste. Against her will, she released an audible sigh.

"Is it okay?" Dace startled her by bringing his head out of his book. "I asked them to make it just the way you like it."

Kerrie's cheeks flushed. "Yes, it's great, thank you." She wondered what the barista, Deenie, was thinking. Would she wonder if they were seeing each other?

"Good," he grinned, before lowering his gaze to his book.

Kerrie hesitated. Perhaps he didn't want to be interrupted?

"Dace," she began. He brought his blue-gray eyes

back to hers. They were gorgeous.

Kerrie went blank. She couldn't remember what she wanted to say. It seemed so hard to focus.

"Yes," he prompted with a charming tilt of his head.

"Oh, nothing," she lost her courage and glanced back down at her book. He probably didn't want to be bothered. He was just there to read.

"What is it, Kerrie? Are you finally ready to talk to me?"

Her eyes flew to his. "What? What do you mean?" she vocalized in a higher than normal pitch.

"Just that I haven't managed to have a conversation with you despite my best efforts over the last 48 hours. So, I've been waiting here patiently until you decided you wanted to talk to me...if you ever did," he finished, with an endearing lopsided grin.

"Oh...I...uh...what did you want to talk about?" she asked uncertainly. "I'm not sure I...I'm fairly quiet...I think." She saw his grin broaden at her incoherency and realized he was chuckling. She heard herself stuttering foolishly and began to laugh with him.

"I'll help you out and get us started," he chuckled gently. "Where are you from?"

Oh, question and answer! She could do this. "A small town in western Washington, you've probably never heard of it."

He nodded, but didn't pursue that question. "Are you married?"

She caught his eye traveling to her left hand. "No," she answered shortly. She fixed her eyes on a shelf of books in the distance. "Are you?"

"No, never been."

"Really?" she asked in surprise, bringing her eyes back to his face.

"Really," he grinned. A muscle twitched in his jaw. "Never found a woman willing to put up with me that long."

Kerrie's eyes narrowed. His response seemed flippant. He had skirted the issue, and rightly so. His personal life was none of her business. Should she ask about Sandy?

"Your turn," he said. "Children?"

"No," she said with a barely concealed sigh. She brightened when she added, "I have a dog, but she's not with me."

"What kind?"

"Oh, some kind of little poodle mix. Suzie. She's with my parents now. I think she's going to stay with them. My dad has become quite attached to her."

"You could have brought her, couldn't you? You're not living in government housing. I would have seen you over there. You live here in town, right?"

How did he know so much about her? Why did he? She retreated into the safety of her seat.

His quick eyes missed nothing. "I'm sorry," he said hastily. "I don't mean to be pry."

She gave him a tentative smile. "That's okay," she relented. "Yes, I'm living here in town. I...I couldn't take Suzie when I left, and it just seems easier to leave her where she is now." She couldn't keep the melancholy out of her voice. "I'm not sure where I'll be in six months or if I can take care of her." She bit her lower lip. *For Pete's sake, shut up, Kerrie. Way too much information. You're babbling.* She looked up to see him watching her with a mixture of sympathy and curiosity, and she was grateful he didn't pursue the subject any further.

"So, how long have you been working for the Park Service?" she asked, pleased to turn the tables on him.

He grinned at her with a knowing smile and answered, "About ten years now. Are you going to stick with it?"

Back to her, darn it. "I'm not sure. I've just started," she favored him with a slight grin. "I'll get back to you in ten years."

As he chuckled, she pressed on. "What did you do before you became a park ranger?"

"Other stuff," he evaded, though he maintained a steady gaze. "College, a white collar job, that sort of thing."

"Really?" she threw in, not quite sure what else to say. What kind of job? What college? What degree? Why did he leave to come to the fairly low-paying Park Service? She dared not ask any of those questions. What if he really pressed her about her past?

"Where are you from originally, Dace?" That seemed like an innocuous question.

"Back east. Virginia. I grew up around Washington, D.C."

Kerrie couldn't hold back the envy in her voice. "I've never been to Washington. I always wanted to go."

He smiled. "So you haven't traveled much?"

She forgot to hold back. "No. I've never really been out of Washington State. Well...one trip to Las Vegas with my parents for my 21st birthday, a trip to Yellowstone when I was a teenager, and now here to Montana." She paused. "Have you traveled a lot?" she asked.

He sighed heavily. "Yeah, it feels like I've been everywhere, but there's always somewhere new to see." He turned his head and looked out the large floor-to-ceiling windows of the reading room. "I can't seem to stop moving," he said pensively. He turned back to her with a slight shake of his head and a wry smile.

"Where have you been?" Kerrie pressed. Keep the focus on him.

"Well, let's see. Europe, Southwest Asia, the Pacific, the Caribbean, and all over the United States. I've worked at most of the big parks, Yellowstone, Yosemite, Great Smokey Mountains, Acadia, the Grand Tetons, and a few of the smaller ones."

Kerrie could only stare in awe. Didn't he miss his family? Where was home now? Was that an appropriate question?

"That's a lot of places. I can't even imagine..." her voice trailed off as she tried to visualize such a life.

His gray eyes narrowed and his jaw tightened at her comment. Had she said something wrong?

"I'm sorry," she offered quickly. "Your life sounds wonderfully adventurous. I didn't mean..."

"It's okay. It's not a life for everyone. A lot of people can't handle it. That's probably why I live alone," he said with a set mouth. Catching her anxious eyes, he gave her a lopsided grin. "It's a good life. I enjoy it."

Kerrie wasn't sure she was convinced, but she said nothing more. What about Sandy? How long had they been together?

"My turn," he said with a speculative gaze in her

direction. "What made you escape to this isolated place?"

Kerrie's eyes flew to his. Was she that obvious?

"Oh, I don't know if I was escaping," she said in her best nonchalant voice. "Lots of people work for the Park Service in seasonal jobs, don't they?"

He nodded, but seemed unconvinced by her airy answer. "Usually college students or retirees or folks who have traveled extensively. None of those fit you."

Think, Kerrie, think. "I sold my house, so I have money put aside." She flashed a bright grin in his direction. "So, I guess that makes me kind of retired."

He narrowed his eyes and nodded skeptically, but to her joy, he didn't press the matter.

Kerrie couldn't take the pressure of the intimate conversation any longer, and she rose from her seat in a tortuous slow *leisurely* fashion. What she really wanted to do was run.

"Well," she tried a yawn behind her hand, "I guess I'd better head home. Early morning and all that." She grinned down at Dace as he made to rise. "Thanks so much for the hot chocolate. I owe you one," she said as she involuntarily backed up when he stood to his full length.

"You're welcome. I'll hold you to it. Goodnight, Kerrie. Sleep well."

She knew he was watching her as she forced each leg in front of the other in the appearance of a stroll, her feet screaming to take off in a run.

She reached her small truck and jumped in, relief easing the constriction in her lungs. She took a deep breath and turned the key in the ignition. Nothing. Just a click.

"Oh no, no, please don't do this, truck."

Several more clicks, and it seemed clear that her truck was not going to start. She fervently hoped it was nothing worse than a dead battery or, better yet, a loose cable.

Please don't come out of the store. Please stay in there and read books for another hour.

She popped the hood and walked around to look at the battery. What did a dead battery look like? It looked very similar to when it was...what? Alive? Active? Working?

She wiggled the cables to the battery, throwing an anxious glance over her shoulder. No Dace. The cables didn't move, which was fine because she didn't have any tools to tighten them anyway.

"What's wrong, Kerrie? Truck won't start?"

Kerrie jumped at the sound of Dace's voice and hit her head on the open hood.

"Ouch," she put a hand to the top of her head.

Dace reached out a hand toward her injured head, and she jumped back with a hand raised in front of her face. He froze in place and stared at her.

Kerrie saw his look of shock, and humiliation swept over her.

"I'm sorry, I'm sorry," she said quickly, struggling to keep hot embarrassed tears from flowing down her face. One slipped out, and she pretended to brush a speck of dust from the offending eye.

"Are you all right?" he finally spoke. He kept his hands firmly at his sides.

She couldn't bear the strange look on his face. She felt like a freak. *I'm not a freak. I'm just...damaged. Don't look at me like that.*

"I'm fine. Just hit my head a bit. Sorry I jumped. Seems like I'm a bit skittish. I really don't know why."

He nodded, again giving her a skeptical look. "Do you want me to take a look at the truck?"

She nodded mutely. He got in the truck and turned the key in the ignition as she had. Click.

He got out and came around the front of the truck to look at the battery connection.

"I think the connections are just a bit dirty. I'll go get something from my truck to clean them."

Kerrie nodded silently again, rubbing the growing knot on her head occasionally. He must think she was a real fruitcake.

Dace returned in a minute with a wrench and battery post scraper. Kerrie had seen them before, but she didn't own one. She vowed to get one. She could do this herself.

Dace cleaned off the battery posts and reattached the cables. He got back in the truck and turned the ignition over. The truck started right up. Kerrie was sure she actually heard it purring under his care.

Dace unfolded his long legs from the small truck and got out.

"There you go," he said with a grin as Kerrie kept her distance.

"Thank you, Dace. I really appreciate your help. I should get one of those gizmos so I don't have to stand by my dead car like a helpless female."

His eyebrows shot up, and he tilted his head inquiringly. "I doubt you're helpless. I've discovered you women are pretty handy when you need to be."

You women? Ah, yes, Sandy.

"Well, thanks again, Dace. I appreciate it. Goodnight."

"Goodnight, Kerrie," he said quietly before he walked off into the dark toward his own truck.

****

Dace climbed in his truck and watched Kerrie pull out of the parking lot. He watched her taillights disappear into the night as he tried to make heads or tails of the evening. What was with that woman? For that matter, what was with him? He had better things to do than stalk an unwilling female. Didn't he?

A vision of his sterile, lonely apartment in government housing popped into view. He hadn't even hooked up cable for television since he'd been there. What was the use? He didn't really like staying in the place anyway. It seemed rather dreary. The review of his travels brought the emptiness of his existence up for examination.

Okay, so maybe he didn't have anything better to do than stalk an unwilling female.

Still, there was something in those beautiful green eyes of hers that compelled him. Every now and then, he caught her looking at him with an expression of...

With a shake of his head and a rueful grin on his face, Dace put the truck into gear and pulled out onto the dark road. Loneliness was turning him into a hopeless romantic, for Pete's sake.

The expression in her eyes when she looked at him. What was it?

Longing?

Dace bit his lower lip. *Nah! Knock it off.* If anything,

Kerrie acted like she would be happy to see the last of him. For the most part.

He smiled at the last thought. There was something about her and he wasn't going to be satisfied until he knew what it was...or she gave him firm marching orders. With a sigh, he pondered the night ahead, hoping he would be able to get some sleep...though that seemed unlikely. The silky dark curls of a complicated woman had been interrupting his sleep for the past few nights.

****

Kerrie arrived at work the next morning, having spent another sleepless night tossing and turning in her bed. Images of Dace frequented her dreams, though she couldn't remember what the dreams were about. When she awakened that morning, she found her extra pillow firmly grasped in her arms. She didn't want to know what her dreams had been about.

Hopelessly enthralled, she was determined to find out some more information about Dace, and she thought she might try asking Sam about him. When Sam came to check on her at the gate, she searched for an opening.

"Morning, Kerrie. You still don't look like you're sleeping well," he said gruffly, with a quick glance at her face.

"I'm not, but I'll be fine, Sam," she reassured him. "It's probably just a temporary thing. You know, getting used to a new place, stuff like that. I won't let it interfere with the job," she said firmly.

"I'm not worried about that. To tell the truth, you have kind of a...a...fragile look about you sometimes. I guess that's the best way to describe it." Sam's weathered face took on a bronze tinge, and he took off his hat and studiously brushed an imaginary speck from the brim.

Kerrie pulled her shoulders back and lifted her chin. "Really? I don't know why that would be. I've never heard that before." She went for humor. "Maybe I'm just getting old," she forced a chuckle. "It's probably just the bags under my eyes from not sleeping."

He looked up at her quickly with a partial grin. "Maybe," he grunted.

"Sam, I was wondering..." A fine time to change the subject. "Umm...I happened to see Dace...you know, the park ranger...at the bookstore last night, and we got to chatting. It sounds like he's traveled as much as you. That must be so fascinating. Have you two met before in any of the other parks?" She hurried on, keeping her eyes on the empty road in front of the gate. "I mean, it seems like National Park Service employees must bump into each other a lot at different parks."

To her dismay, Sam crossed his arms and leaned against the wall of the gate shack. She was pretty sure his smile could be best described as a smirk.

"Yeah, I know Dace. Have for years." Sam kept his twinkling blue eyes on her face and offered no more information.

"Oh," Kerrie struggled for a return. "Oh, well, of course. You must meet other employees all the time in your travels."

"Yeah, you mentioned that." His smirk grew. "Why do you ask?"

"Oh, no reason. I was just curious, that's all. Just trying to get to know people," she announced triumphantly. That sounded good.

"Mary and I have known Dace for ten years now, ever since he started with the Park Service. Mary was his first supervisor." He grinned mischievously at her. "Is there something specific you wanted to know about him? The women always do," he finished with a chuckle and a shake of his head.

"Oh no, I was just wondering. No, not me." She held up an implausible hand in stop sign fashion. "I'm not interested in men...no, I don't mean that. I mean, no...I'm not asking about him like that. I was just curious—"

"Okay, Kerrie, you can stop stuttering. You'll make me start quoting Shakespeare and "methinks" and "doth protest too much" and all that. Now, do I look like the kind of man who quotes Shakespeare?"

Kerrie broke out into a full-bodied laugh which felt refreshing and invigorating. Sam dropped his arms and chuckled along with her.

"No, Sam, somehow you don't look like the kind of guy who quotes Shakespeare." She wiped tears of laughter from her eyes.

"Okay, I've got to take off and check on everyone

else," he said as he headed out the door. "If you're really curious about Dace, you might ask Sandy. She knows him pretty well." He let the door shut, got in his park truck, and drove off.

The tears of laughter froze on her cheeks. Sandy! Had Sam deliberately introduced her name to put Kerrie in her place? That sort of thing didn't seem like the gruff but kind man. She clamped her mouth shut. She had no intention of asking Sandy about Dace. Sandy, a woman, would know in a heartbeat that Kerrie had a crush on her man.

Kerrie didn't see Dace that day, and she was unaccountably irritable when she arrived home. She had just made herself a sandwich for dinner when the phone rang.

"Hi, honey, how are you? Are you settling in?"

"Hi, Mom," Kerrie was pleased to hear her mother's familiar voice. "I'm fine. Settling in." She looked around the small sparsely furnished apartment. Nothing in it was hers. "As best I can," she said wistfully.

"You sound homesick, hon. I wish you were here."

"So do I, Mom, but I'm enjoying myself here. The job is fun and the people are nice."

"Kerrie," her mother began hesitantly.

"Yes?" Kerrie knew that tone. Her mother was about to broach an unpleasant subject. It could only be one of three things, a family member, her dog, or...

"He called here looking for you," her mom said in a low voice.

Chapter Four

Kerrie's hand froze on the phone. Her heart began to pound and she involuntarily held her breath.

"When?" she asked in a croaking whisper.

"Today. I couldn't believe it was him on the phone. I didn't tell him anything, of course, but he knows you left town."

"How? Why? How could he know?" The familiar anxiety began to suffocate her. She struggled to draw air into her lungs.

"He found out that you sold the house, and I guess the realtor told him he thought you had moved away. He doesn't know where you are though. The realtor told him to contact us as this was your forwarding address.

"What did he say?" she asked reluctantly.

"Oh, Kerrie, you know him. He says everything he's supposed to and nothing close to the truth." Loathing colored her mother's usual sweet voice. "He asked how you were and said he still loved you. He said he misses you and that he's sorry." Her mother paused. "I didn't really want to tell you what he said, but it's your right to hear it...if you want."

"That's okay, Mom. It's nothing I haven't heard before. He hasn't changed," Kerrie said in a tired voice. "It doesn't matter anyway. It's finally over, thank goodness."

"I'm so glad," her mother agreed fervently.

"So, what did you tell him, anyway?" She wasn't sure she wanted to know.

"I told him that you had moved and I didn't know where you'd gone. I'm sure he doesn't believe me, but I don't care," her mother said defiantly. "I asked him not to call again."

Kerrie winced as she heard the disgust in her mother's voice as she repudiated the man Kerrie once loved. "And what did he say to that?" Kerrie asked quietly.

"He said he was sorry for bothering me and asked me to pass on the message if I should hear from you. That's all," she finished dismissively.

A familiar wave of pain and loss swept over Kerrie. When would it be over? When would it stop hurting?

"Mom, I know you don't want to hear this, but I left him because of what he was doing, not because I didn't love him once. I haven't forgotten." Kerrie struggled to keep her voice steady. "It still hurts."

"I know, Kerrie, I know. I just can't understand how you could have ever loved that man. But I know it doesn't make it any easier to say goodbye." Her mother paused. "It *is* over, isn't it, Kerrie?"

Kerrie stiffened and sat up straight in her chair. "Yes, Mom, it most definitely is *over*. I'm not going back...ever."

"I'm glad, dear. It took forever for you to leave. I began to think you never would." She sighed. "Well, I'd better get off the phone and start dinner. I'll call you again tomorrow, honey. Take care. I love you."

"You too, Mom. I love you too. Night," Kerrie said quietly. Her apartment had grown dark, and with a shiver, she jumped up to turn on some lamps. She hugged her arms around herself and wondered what to do. A growing uneasiness permeated her consciousness, and she wanted to run from it. She wanted to feel safe again.

Hot chocolate and a warm, safe and cocooning chair in the well-lit bookstore surrounded by people. That's what she needed!

****

Within half an hour, Kerrie was securely ensconced in a chair, sipping on a hot chocolate. She left her book unopened on her lap and relaxed her head against the pillowed chair back while she gazed with half-closed eyes up at the high acoustic ceiling. Hard won serenity overcame the underlying current of anxiety in her body, and she melted further into the nest of her chair.

Everything would be okay. She would live. After all, no one ever really died of a broken heart. If anything, she had probably added years to her life by leaving. The bad stuff was over.

She was so involved in her self-talk that she didn't

hear Dace approach.

"Are you talking to yourself? You're staring at the ceiling and your lips are moving," he chuckled, as he sat down in the seat next to hers. He still wore his Park Service uniform.

Kerrie wasn't surprised to see him there, but she was startled at the enthusiasm in her voice as she greeted him.

"Hi, Dace, it's good to see you."

Dace's gray eyes widened and he blinked. "It's good to see you too, Kerrie."

She put a hand to a warm cheek as she tried to tone down her greeting. What was that about? She knew he looked fabulous in his uniform, but he wasn't a knight in shining armor. Well, he wasn't her knight in shining armor. He might be Sandy's.

"I wanted to thank you once again for helping me with my car. It was very kind of you," she said in a more formal tone.

"You're welcome...once again," he chuckled. "How was your day today? I didn't see you."

"Good, fine, thank you. How about yours?"

He shrugged. "Okay, nothing special." He paused for a moment before continuing. "Listen, Kerrie, I was wondering..."

"Yes?" *Uh oh, what does he want to know?* Her body involuntarily tightened.

"You look worried," he chuckled. "I'm not going to pry. I think there are some things you don't want to talk about, and that's okay...for now. I was wondering if you wanted to get something to eat, that's all."

"Like...like d-dinner?" she stuttered.

"Yeah, dinner. There aren't a lot of places to eat here in town, but there's a little bar and grill called *The Keg* that whips up a pretty mean burger. I'm starved. Would you like to go with me?"

"Oh..." she said nonplussed. "Um...okay. I don't think I ate dinner either," she said as she remembered the telephone call from her mother. What about...Sandy? Would she mind?

"Good." He rose and reached out a hand to help her up. She reluctantly put a moist hand in his. Her hand was sweating. "Thanks," she said, pulling her hand away quickly and wiping it on the side of her jeans.

"I washed my hands," he said with a slight narrowing of his gray-blue eyes.

"Oh, no. I know that. Well, no, I don't know that...but..." *Speak, Kerrie, speak.* She took a deep breath and explained. "I'm sorry. My hand was sweating. So embarrassing," she murmured as she rubbed it on her leg again.

He grinned and grabbed her hand again. "I hadn't noticed. Let's go eat." He led the way out of the store and towed her along towards his truck.

"I could drive my truck and meet you there," she protested futilely as she stared longingly at her own truck. So simple, so uncomplicated.

He paused at the passenger door of his truck and looked down at her. "I'd like to drive you. I'll bring you back in a few hours. Okay?" He grinned. "I'll even wait around to see if you need another jump."

She returned his smirk with one of her own. "Very funny. Okay, you drive. It'll be nice to be a passenger for a while. I can't remember the last time someone drove me somewhere." She hopped into the truck and he closed the door behind her.

He was a confident driver, and Kerrie relaxed into the cloth-covered seat of his truck. They were silent on the way to the restaurant. Within a few minutes, they had arrived at a small one-story white building with a bright red neon sign perched above it. *The Keg, Fine Family Dining.*

Dace pulled into one of the last remaining spots, and Kerrie jumped down from the truck before he could come around to open her door. She met him at the front of the truck.

"I've seen this place before, but I've never been here. It looks packed," she said as she stuffed her hands in her jeans pockets.

Dace put a hand on her back and guided her forward. "The food is great. I love eating here. It usually is crowded, but we won't have to wait. This is Columbia Falls. We don't have the big city waits here," he grinned down at her.

Kerrie smiled back up at him, but she was distracted by the feel of his hand on her back. The warmth felt wonderful in the small of her back. She pulled her hands out of her pockets. Had she hidden them so he wouldn't take her hand? She wasn't sure.

Dace held the door open for her and she preceded him into a crowded restaurant notable for its 1950s style red vinyl booths and plastic red checkered cloths on the smaller tables.

"Well, look what the wind blew in. How ya doing, Dace? Who's this?" A high-energy, short and stout woman with close-cropped red hair bustled forward, wiping her hands on a black apron. She grabbed a few menus from the register while she studied Kerrie appraisingly.

"Evening, Sally. This is Kerrie. She's new at the Park. This is her first year."

"Welcome, Kerrie. Are you from Montana?" Sally threw over her shoulder as she led them to a booth.

"No, I'm from Washington," Kerrie answered briefly. What a small town this was! Apparently, everyone knew everyone. She had hoped for a little more anonymity. She followed Sally, acutely aware of Dace close behind. She reached up a self-conscious hand to smooth her hair in back.

"We're neighbors then. You'll love it here. I've lived here all my life." She laid the menus down at an empty booth. "I'll get some water for you." She paused. "Hey, Dace. Tell Sandy I got those pictures developed from her birthday party. They're a hoot. She can pick them up anytime. Maybe Saturday morning if you guys are having breakfast here." She bustled away, never knowing the turmoil her words created in Kerrie's psyche.

Kerrie buried her red face behind the oversized plastic menu. How embarrassing! So, Dace and Sandy *were* dating. Then what was she doing there? She felt foolish and ignorant. Was this normal behavior these days? Date one woman and eat dinner with another?

"That *was* quite the party. They had it late after closing last Friday night. It was a surprise party. One of Sandy's friends set it up for her."

Kerrie could hear him speaking from the other side of her menu and she reluctantly lowered it to face him. He studied his menu as well and shook his head with a grin. He looked up at her with warm gray eyes. He continued to smile widely, so she knew the smile plastered on her face appeared normal. She forced her eyes to relax and met his gaze with a round-eyed one of her own.

"Sounds like it," she murmured, seemingly intent on the huge selection of food displayed on her menu. "So, what do you usually eat here?"

"The triple-decker cheeseburger with homemade fries. Once a week whether I need it or not," he patted his flat stomach and winked at her.

She stiffened slightly. Jack used to wink like that. A pang of longing for the familiar washed over her...even if it had been a nightmare.

"Is everything all right? Your face..."

"Oh, sure. I'm fine. Just wondering what to eat, that's all." She busied herself with running her finger up and down the items on the menu. "Let's see. A salad. That sounds nice."

"For rabbits, I guess," he gave her a lop-sided grin.

She put the past behind her and focused on the present. "Call me Bugs," she returned his grin with a crooked one of her own.

"So, what are you going to have?" Sally arrived with her pad in hand. They gave her their orders and made light conversation about Columbia Falls and the Park Service until their food arrived. Her salad arrived on a huge platter with slices of French bread. She was sure she couldn't eat it all.

"How's your salad?" Dace asked after she had taken a few bites.

"Good," she replied. "It's—"

"Well, there you are," Sandy said as she slid into the booth next to Dace. "I've been looking everywhere for you. Do you mind if I join you all?"

Dace nonchalantly moved over to give her room. Kerrie choked down some lettuce and grinned toothily. Guiltily, she peeked at Sandy's face. Was she angry?

"Hi, Sandy," she chirped. "I saw Dace in the bookstore and he said he was coming to eat, so I came along. I've never been here. It's a nice restaurant, isn't it?" she babbled.

Sandy favored Kerrie with a generous smile of perfect white teeth. She reached over to ruffle Dace's dark hair. He batted her hand away teasingly, but continued to chew his food.

"He loves that bookstore. It seems like he's always there these days. You didn't hardly ever go there last year, did you?" She waved at a few people in the restaurant. "What do you think I should have, Dace? I'm starving."

"The usual," he replied briefly.

Kerrie's eyes flickered back and forth between them. She didn't want to be caught staring. Dace had taken Sandy's arrival in stride, showing no surprise or embarrassment. Well, that was okay for him. Kerrie had plenty of guilt for both of them. Dace was friendly, but seemed undemonstrative. Somehow, Kerrie had thought he would be more romantic. She lowered her gaze to her food. It wasn't like she was any great judge of character anyway. Maybe the romantic ones were the most dangerous.

"Sounds good." She called out to Sally who passed by with a tray of food. "Club sandwich for me, Sally."

"Coming up," Sandy answered.

"That's a huge salad," Sandy leaned forward on her elbows and peered at Kerrie's food. "Is it good?"

Kerrie nodded mutely and stuffed more lettuce into her mouth.

"Sally said she's got the pictures from the party for you," Dace said.

"Oh really? I can't wait to see them." She rose and went toward the kitchen.

Kerrie looked over at Dace, but could think of nothing to say. She chased the last few pieces of lettuce around her plate hoping to look too busy for conversation.

"I didn't know she was coming," Dace said. He tilted his head and favored her with a speculative gaze. "By the way, I'm pretty sure I invited you to eat. I don't recall anything about you *tagging along*."

"Oh, really? Well, I was just saying..."

"Are you guys talking about me?" Sandy asked with a teasing grin as she sat back down. She had a package of photos in her hand and pulled them out to review. She handed some to Dace and a few to Kerrie. As they reviewed the photos, Sandy laughed often, pointing the occasional one out to Dace for discussion.

Kerrie watched Sandy's blonde head bent close to Dace's dark one. They made a beautiful couple, complementing each other so well, both tall, one dark, one fair. It was no wonder they were together.

She cast a cursory glance at the photos in her hand. Balloons, a radiant and laughing Sandy, a birthday cake, Dace leaning on the bar. She didn't recognize any of the people in her set of pictures.

"These are hilarious," Sandy giggled. "That was a fun party. Let's do this again next year."

Dace looked over at her and shook his head. "Not me, dear."

"What? Oh yeah, I forgot," Sandy shook her head though she continued to chuckle. She took the photos back from Kerrie and Dace and put them away. Her food arrived promptly and she ate with a hearty appetite, obviously having no need to watch her weight.

Kerrie listened with interest as Dace and Sandy discussed activities in the Park. While they both directed comments toward Kerrie and included her in the conversation, she knew she listened to seasoned veterans of the Park Service and she had nothing to contribute but naiveté and questions. She found herself distracted from the subject by speculations about their relationship.

They communicated well together with an ease that spoke of a longer-term relationship than Kerrie previously thought. They appeared to be of similar intelligence and tastes, though Sandy was considerably younger than Dace. Kerrie felt like an old woman next to her...a short old woman.

"Kerrie?"

Kerrie realized she had been staring at Sandy. Her face reddened.

"What?"

Sandy chuckled and waved her hand near Kerrie's face. "Earth to Kerrie. Where'd you go?"

"I'm sorry. I just faded out. It's been a long day, I guess." Kerrie kept her eyes averted from Dace.

"I was asking if you're working tomorrow." Sandy

leaned back in the booth and stretched her shapely arms over her head. "I'm heading home. I'm pooped."

"Oh, yes, yes, I am." Kerry busied herself with her napkin.

"Well, good, I'll see you then. I guess Dace is going to take you back to your truck, so I'll say goodnight."

She leaned over and kissed Dace on the cheek before rising. "Hey, grab the check for me, will you?"

"Was there ever a doubt?" Dace murmured as she moved away without waiting for a response. He turned to Kerrie who felt completely awkward and out of place.

"Do you want dessert? They have great huckleberry ice cream here." He grinned before taking a sip of his coffee.

"No, thanks," she murmured. What an odd couple! She wasn't at all sure she would have left her man with a strange woman...if she had a man.

"You do look beat," he commiserated. "Are you ready to go?"

Kerrie kept her eyes on the table and nodded her head, anxious to be out of the strange situation and away from Dace's irresistible spell.

He rose from the table, and Kerrie sprang up to follow him to the cash register. She pulled out her wallet, but he put a staying hand on her arm. She opened her mouth to protest, but he narrowed his eyes and gave her a slight shake of his head.

"Don't," he said quietly.

To her surprise, Kerrie obediently put her wallet back in her purse, forgoing her usual insistence on paying her way.

"How was the food, honey?" Sally busily rang up the ticket and took Dace's money.

"Good, Sally, as always."

"Glad to hear it. Bring the little gal back, Dace. See you soon." With a swish and a bustle, she vanished toward the kitchen.

Dace held the door for Kerrie who moved through it silently. He followed her out to the truck and strode past her to grab the door, which she had reached out to open.

"I've got it," he chuckled.

"Thanks, I could have..."

"Yes, I know you would have opened it yourself. Allow me." The lights of the restaurant reflected his white-toothed grin. "Kind of on the independent side, aren't you, Kerrie?"

She climbed in the truck. What could she say to that? Nothing particularly witty came to mind at the moment. In fact, her thoughts bordered on chaotic.

"Life makes you like that sometimes."

Dace closed the door and leaned his outstretched arms against it for a moment, staring at her. She turned her face away from him and toward the bright lights spilling out of the restaurant windows, wishing he would back up, yet savoring his masculine smell.

"It does, doesn't it?" His low spoken words seemed genuine, empathetic.

He pushed away from the truck and came around the front to climb into the driver's seat. With a sideways glance in Kerrie's direction, which she did not miss, he started the engine, put the truck in gear, and pulled out of the parking lot.

Kerrie breathed deep on the short drive back to her truck. She wanted to take in his scent before she had to give him back to Sandy, to keep it with her through the long lonely days ahead. In a perfect world, Dace was a man she could have loved, but he belonged to someone else. At any rate, she didn't know if she could ever trust a man enough to love again.

Dace pulled up to her truck and came around to her side. Kerrie had already jumped down by the time he got there and he shook his head and chuckled.

"You can't blame a guy for trying to do the right thing, can you?"

Kerrie grinned. "I may be short, but I'm fast."

"You are that." He put his hands on his blue-jeaned hips. "Well, I know something you *do* need me for. Why don't you go turn that truck of yours on and let's see if it starts?"

Kerrie tossed her brown curls. "I'm sure it will. I really am going to get one of those battery cable cleaning things. It's ridiculous to have to call a man for help for every little thing." She moved away toward her truck, delightfully aware he followed. She hopped in and willed her truck to start. It did. She lowered the window to thank Dace.

He leaned down and rested his hands on her door.

"Well, shoot, the darn thing started," he teased. "Now, I'm just not much good for anything, am I?"

Kerrie's eyes widened and she hurried to demur. "Oh no, I'm grateful you helped me with the truck and showed me the restaurant. I didn't mean to make you feel bad."

"I was just kidding, Kerrie." He touched his fingers to his mouth and brushed them gently against her nose. "By they way, I took you out to dinner. That's a little bit different than *showing you a restaurant*." He grinned. "Good night. I'll see you at work." He turned away before she could squeak out an appropriate farewell. He climbed into his truck, turned on the engine and lights, and waited

Kerrie longed to rub the spot on her nose that he had touched, but she could see that he was going to wait until she left.

She pulled out of the parking lot, hoping he wouldn't *see her home*. She didn't want him to know where she lived. He followed her out of the parking lot, and she made the first right, but Dace kept going...probably back to housing at the Park.

Kerrie made her way home and dashed into her apartment, making a beeline for the bathroom. She flipped on the switch and stared at her nose. Had he really kissed his fingers and then her nose? Or had he just tapped her nose in a playful brotherly fashion? The latter seemed likely as the image of Sandy's beautiful face came into view.

She brushed her teeth and made ready for bed, wondering again about the relationship between Dace and Sandy. It seemed of long standing, but very casual. Well, Sandy knew she had nothing to worry about. She probably knew that every day she looked in her mirror.

Kerrie climbed into bed and fluffed her pillow. She closed her eyes and quickly moved toward that precipice just before sleep, when her cell phone on the night table rang.

Dace! She groggily reached for the phone, her eyes blurring as she tried to read the backlit caller ID.

Unknown number. Confused by sleep and a vivid imagination that suggested Dace would be calling her, she answered the phone.

"Hello?"

Silence.

The room lay in darkness, not even a sliver of moonlight peeped through the curtains. She looked at the phone again. The call was still connected.

"Hello?"

Silence.

Kerrie's heart began a familiar racing, a sickening feeling she hoped never to experience again.

She stared at the intrusive bright light in her hand, indicating the caller had not hung up. She slammed the phone shut. Reaching blindly in the dark, she found the table lamp and turned it on. The phone in her hand seemed innocuous, a small thing which in itself posed no threat, but she stared at it as if it were a cobra.

Jack! There seemed little doubt. It was Jack.

Chapter Five

Kerrie stood at the gate the following day, grateful for the busy visitor traffic that kept her mind occupied. She'd slept little the night before, agitation and a sense of unease preventing her from getting any rest. Perhaps she overreacted in the dark of night. Unknown numbers continued to be quite common if the phone carrier did not recognize the number. Though she'd never had an unknown caller on her new cell phone. The only people with her number were her parents and work.

"Good morning. How are you?" she plastered a welcoming smile on her face.

"Great! We're excited to be here. What do we need to know?" The carload of happy vacationers lifted Kerrie's spirits. Her concerns flew out the window in the face of the excitement and hope of tourists on their first visit to Glacier National Park.

She took their money and handed them a pass.

"Here is your guide and a map. Have a wonderful visit." Kerrie waved to the bouncing children in the back seat and adjusted her hat just in time for the next car. The Park saw more and more visitors every day.

A sultry voice came over the intercom. "Are you doing okay out there?"

Sandy! Kerrie pushed the button.

"Oh yeah, everything's fine. Happy visitors."

"That's what we like to hear. I'll relieve you in a half hour for lunch."

"Okay," Kerrie let the intercom go and turned to face the next vehicle approaching. She swallowed hard when she saw the white SUV with the National Park Service logo and green stripe running down the side...a ranger.

It could be any number of rangers. They all stopped by the gate to visit.

"Good morning, Kerrie. How are you this morning?" Dace pulled his sunglasses off, forcing Kerrie to meet his seductive blue-gray eyes. She backed up as had become her habit. His dark lashed eyes flickered momentarily, but he continued to smile.

"I don't bite," he murmured.

"No, no, I'm sure you don't," she stammered. "Uh...I'm fine. How are you?"

"Good. Did you sleep well?" One tanned hand rested on steering wheel and the other lay on the door in the open window.

Kerrie blinked. How did he know? She gave herself a mental shake. He didn't. The question was common.

"Yes, fine."

"You're shaking your head. Is everything all right?" Dace's sharp eyes narrowed.

"What? Oh yeah. Did I shake my head? I'm probably just trying to wake up." Kerrie favored him with a friendly grin...at least she hoped it looked friendly.

Dace tilted his head, studying her, probing her innermost secrets.

"Well, um...Sandy is inside."

He gave her a curious look and nodded. "Thanks. I can't stop for a visit. I've got some sort of bear sighting to respond to."

"Really?" Kerrie couldn't keep the awe from her voice.

"Yeah, I'm the bear ranger. Didn't I tell you?"

Kerrie shook her head, completely bowled over with hero worship. No longer wonderfully handsome and extremely kind, Dace had suddenly transformed himself into a god...that most mysterious of all Park Service employees...*a bear ranger.*

"Wow!" she squeaked, unable to stop groveling at his feet.

His eyes flickered and he dropped them momentarily, a bronze hue flushed his cheeks.

"Not that big of a thing, really."

"So, what's the bear sighting today? What do you have to do?" In her excitement, Kerrie gripped the edge of the window and unconsciously leaned forward. Aware of her movements, she couldn't pull back.

"Just a grizzly sow and two cubs wandering near a campground. She'll probably behave. It's the bear-loving tourists I'm worried about." His radio squawked. "That's for me. I'd better get going. I'll let you know how it goes."

He drove away, leaving Kerrie with an empty hand raised in farewell and feeling not just a little foolish as she stared after him. She sank back onto her stool and adjusted her hat once more. Her heart rate slowed and she finally came back to reality with a glance toward the office. Hopefully, no one saw her panting after the man...especially Sandy. She looked up at the camera. The black and white screen inside the office couldn't possibly reveal the flush on her face.

"Hey, there. Was that Dace?" Sandy's voice came over the intercom.

Kerrie gulped. "Ummm...yeah. He said he couldn't stop and visit. Had to go due to a bear sighting."

"Oh, drat! Okay. I'll be out in a minute."

Sandy walked over within minutes, her hat perched dashingly on her blonde hair, long, lithe frame virtually modeling the National Park Service uniform. She exchanged drawers with Kerrie, who backed out of the small kiosk.

"So, did he say what kind of bear sighting?"

Kerrie prayed she wouldn't sound ignorant. "Ummm, a grizzly sow and her cubs? Over by Apgar Campground?"

Sandy nodded. "Ah, she's been around for a few weeks. I hope she moves out on her own. She can't stay around here forever. Too many people. Bad combination."

Kerrie nodded sagely, soaking up as much information as she could.

"I didn't know Dace was a bear ranger."

Sandy waved an employee vehicle through and turned back to Kerrie, who stalled at the opposite window of the kiosk. She raised delicate eyebrows.

"Really? Hmmm. Well, he is, has been for...oh...about five years now. I remember when he went to training."

Kerrie's heart dropped. So Sandy and Dace had been together for at least five years. That relationship seemed set in stone. Not that Kerrie wanted to break the relationship up, nor was it within her power to do so.

"Really?" she murmured, the image of Dace's face swimming out of view as he followed Sandy down a path toward a mythological rainbow.

"Yeah...and he's seen some action, let me tell you."

Sandy's eyebrows rose again.

Kerrie shifted from foot to foot. "Wow. I'd love to hear about it sometime. You'll have to tell me. I'd better get inside and finish the paperwork for my shift."

"Okay. Dace could tell his stories better than I could repeat them. Ask him."

"Uh, sure," Kerrie mumbled as she moved away. Sure. She'd just run right up to him and pester him like a lovelorn fan. Not likely. She straightened her shoulders and entered the office to work on her paperwork.

Two shifts later, she removed her hat for the last time that day and laid it on the back seat of her truck. She looked forward to the weekend and a hike she had mapped out for herself. An able-bodied person didn't come to Glacier National Park and not hike...or so she'd heard. With virtually no hiking experience, she picked a fairly easy...and safe...hike to a place called Avalanche Lake—a popular destination for visitors to the Park.

****

Dace drove away from the kiosk with one eye on the road ahead and the other to the rear. Kerrie leaned out and watched him.

Good, he thought. Anything to get her attention. He wasn't getting very far with her, and frankly, he wasn't sure why he kept trying.

He chewed the inside of his lower lip for a moment, knowing that was a lie. He kept trying because she held him in thrall. He couldn't get enough of her. Maybe it was a case of "you want what you can't have," because the woman's eyes said one thing, but her words said another.

He didn't miss the little bit of admiration in her eyes when he mentioned being the bear ranger. In fact, he'd felt his face turn red.

Well, he thought with a rueful smile, whatever it takes to get her attention. If he had to play up Ranger Rick... Well, he wasn't opposed to doing that.

Dace sighed as he neared the campground. Cars lined up alongside the road, impeding traffic. Visitors emerged from the vehicles in hopes of seeing the bear and her cubs, who reportedly foraged in the woods 100 yards from the road. He pulled over, climbed out of the vehicle, and went about the duties of rounding up tourists who pestered feeding bears.

****

Kerrie's phone rang again in the middle of the night, startling her from a deep sleep. She grabbed the phone. *Unknown caller.* With a dry mouth and pounding heart, she jabbed the button to turn off the phone and shoved it in her nightstand drawer. She rolled over on her back and stared up at the dark ceiling.

What if Jack found her number? What were the chances he would soon follow?

Kerrie tossed the covers aside restlessly, at once hot, then freezing. She grabbed them and pulled them back up to her chin.

It couldn't be Jack. He had no way of knowing where she hid. Her parents would never let that information slip. They knew what was at stake. They, more than anyone, wanted Jack out of her life, begging her to obtain a restraining order until she finally gave in.

He didn't know where she was. He couldn't know. She closed her eyes and willed herself back to sleep, replacing the frantic thoughts with visions of her upcoming hike. As she drifted off again, she imagined Dace standing next to Jack, both men so tall—one so charming yet so violent, the other charming but unknown...and therefore dangerous.

When Kerrie woke up the next morning, she dug into her drawer for her cell phone and turned it back on, holding it away from her face as if it might sting her. A sideways peek revealed no further calls in the night and no voice mails. Thank goodness. It could have been as innocent as some company trying to sell her something. Although late night hours seemed like a bad time to call.

She packed up a sandwich, grabbed some water to throw in her backpack, and bounced out the door, happy to finally get time off to enjoy the Park. Chipper, the chipmunk, rested on the hood of her truck, and she clapped her hands to shoo him away.

"Off you go, Chipper. I've got plans today and you can't come. Maybe I'll bring you a snack later. Some peanuts?"

She jumped into the truck and made her way onto the highway in high spirits. Spring had sprung and the trees along the highway and the river sported full growth—bright green, fluttering leaves that seemed to wave at her as she drove past. She pulled into the Park entrance and slowed at the gate. Traffic was light since her weekend fell on Tuesdays and Wednesdays. James manned the visitor's entrance.

"Good morning, James," she sang on a cheery note.

He blinked. "Good morning, Kerrie. I didn't recognize you. You look different without your uniform on."

Kerrie blushed, hoping that passed for a compliment. "I should hope so. I'm off to go hiking today...my first time." She grinned with anticipation.

"Where are you headed?" He returned her grin.

"Avalanche Lake," she boasted.

"Ah, everyone likes that one. Well, that's a good starter hike." He leaned down to whisper. "Do you have any bear spray with you?"

Kerrie gulped. "Bear spray? Are you kidding?"

"No, Kerrie. You really ought to have some."

"Good gravy. I thought...since this was a popular hike."

"Well, you probably won't need any on this hike, but still, you should always carry some when you hike in Glacier."

"I-I don't have any on me."

"Dace is working. I saw him go through a few minutes ago. Why don't you pull over and I'll call and ask him to bring you some? They always have extra in the patrol cars."

"What?" she squeaked. "No, oh no, I couldn't trouble... No."

"He won't mind. We can't have our employees eaten by bears." James snickered in a high nasal tone.

"James," Kerrie reprimanded. "I'll be fine. I'll take some spray out with me next time, okay?"

"Okay, sister. You can lead a horse to water, but you can't make her carry spray." He threw back his head and guffawed.

"Uh...see you later, James. If I'm not at work in two days, I got eaten by a bear." Kerrie shook her head in amused exasperation and waved as she drove off.

The last thing she needed was an encounter with

Dace on her day off. She looked forward to getting outdoors and immersing herself in the rhythm of nature with its sights and sounds, the smell and feel of the cool air, surrounding trees, foliage, birds, squirrels, streams and waterfalls.

Kerrie soon arrived at the trailhead, parked and hopped out of her truck. She strapped on her backpack, rolled up the sleeves of her tan cotton shirt, and set off down the path...or more aptly...up the path. The path took an immediate climb above a spectacular body of water called Avalanche Creek. She neared the edge and peered over to witness a sight too beautiful to describe—silky, glossy water rushed down from a waterfall and over colorful rounded rocks, narrowing and calming as it progressed downstream. She put down her bag and extracted her small camera from it in a futile attempt to capture the glory in a still frame. With one hand braced on a tree, she took photo after photo of the majestic waterfall, wondering how many gallons of water pulsed through the narrow channel before it fell on the rocks below.

With a sigh, she stowed her camera and moved up the path. She exchanged greetings with occasional visitors on their way back down to the parking lot. The trail continued to climb, and she found herself gasping for breath all too soon. Her previous employment as a school teacher had not prepared her for 500-foot elevation gains, although chasing five-year olds all day could be fairly arduous.

The little ones would have loved the fairy-tale forest path along which she now trod. She missed their shining little faces, but Jack's unwelcome harassing visits to the school forced her to resign for the children's sake.

She shook her head to dispel the images and inhaled deeply. The scent of pine trees and damp earth enveloped her. She realized she hadn't passed any other hikers in the last ten minutes. Away from the river, the noises of the forest amplified the crunch of leaves under her feet, the chirping of the birds, a slight breeze whistling through a tree, an occasional rustle in the undergrowth.

With a catch in her breath, Kerrie turned in the direction of one such rustle. Why hadn't she done the sensible thing and wait for some bear spray? A movement in the bushes caught her attention and she froze. Nothing appeared. She wracked her brain trying to remember what to do in the event of a bear encounter. Freeze, run, scream, huddle in the fetal position. They all sounded right.

She pushed herself to move, nervously taking longer strides. The path finally leveled out, but she caught her feet on the occasional tree root. A sound behind her startled her. She turned, but saw nothing around the bend in the path. She faced forward again and sped up to a slow trot, hoping to meet other hikers soon. The sound behind her grew closer, louder. Rapid steps approached. Terrified, Kerrie took off at a run, a sob escaping her lips.

"Kerrie."

A voice stopped her in her tracks and she swung around.

Dace came around the bend in the path, a hand waved in greeting.

"Wait up. Have you been running? What's wrong?"

Kerrie opened her mouth to speak, but to her dismay, a sob erupted.

"I-I thought you were..." She panted, her knees weak.

Dace grabbed her arms as she wobbled. "You thought I was...a bear."

She nodded dumbly, as he led her to a rock and forced her to sit.

"Where's your bear spray?" He braced one foot on the rock, leaned on his bent knee, and stared down at her with narrowed eyes and a set mouth. The severity of his expression brought another face to mind. She cringed.

"I-I don't have any."

"Well, you should. Here, take mine." He handed her a small red canister encased by a black carrying strap. She reached for it with a shaky hand.

"You're shaking, Kerrie. What's wrong? Still worried about a bear?"

She dragged in a deep breath, the bear no longer her concern. He towered above her, his foot on the rock so close to her hip, the memory of his severe tone nerve wracking.

"No, I'm good." She tried to make sense of the chaos

in her mind. "You-you're just so tall." She kept a wary eye on his foot.

The foot dropped to the ground and Dace crouched down in front of her, taking her free hand in his.

"I'm sorry. I don't mean to scare you."

Kerrie raised troubled eyes to his gray ones. She tried to pull her hand from his, but he held onto it...gently, but firmly.

"What is it, Kerrie? What scares you?" His eyes searched her face, but she gritted her teeth and stiffened her spine, denying him the truth.

"Nothing...everything," she twisted her lips into a grin. "Don't worry about me. I'm fine." Kerrie rose slowly and stared up the path. "I'd better get going if I'm going to get there and back down anytime today."

"I'm going with you," he announced.

"Dace! You don't have to do that. I'm fine. Look, there are some hikers coming now." A young couple returning from the lake passed them with a cheery wave.

"Not too much further. You can do it. It's all downhill on the way back." The young girl sent encouraging words their way.

Dace gave them a friendly wave.

"Are you ready? Do you want me to lead the way?"

"Aren't you supposed to be working?" Kerrie muttered.

"I am. I'm checking out a bear sighting near Avalanche Lake as it happens. A good reason for you to carry bear spray."

"Oh," relief swept over her. "I thought James had sent you up here to check on me. He threatened to."

Dace, striding ahead of her, called over his shoulder. "He did. I came up here to find you."

Kerrie paused momentarily before rushing to catch up. "I thought you said you were checking out a bear sighting."

Dace turned and grinned over his shoulder without breaking stride. "I am. Someone reported seeing a black bear up here yesterday. We don't usually investigate black bear sightings unless the bear seemed threatening, but I thought I'd come on up anyway."

"Oh." Kerrie hurried along in his wake, unable to

avoid admiring the curve of his backside and the muscles of his legs flexing through the green jeans of his uniform. She delighted in the view and cursed herself for ogling another woman's man.

"Did you see Sandy?" She called out breathlessly. He really did hike at a rapid pace.

"Sandy? Not since dinner the night before. Why?"

"Oh." Kerrie could have kicked herself. That was her third pointless *oh* in a row. "Just wondering."

"We're almost there."

Suddenly, the trees thinned and they emerged onto the shore of a beautiful pristine blue lake surrounded by snow-capped mountains. The lake resembled a small version of Crater Lake, which she'd seen in photos. Kerrie moved ahead of Dace and picked her way quickly across the pebble beach till she reached the edge of the water. Several rough-hewn logs were fashioned into benches, and she dropped her pack onto one. She dug out her camera and snapped several photos until satisfied she had captured the vista. She turned to see Dace lower himself onto the bench, stretching his legs out in front with his hands resting behind his head.

"Tourist," she indicated the camera and grinned.

"Yes, you are," he smiled lazily. "It's kind of cute."

Kerrie glanced at him uncertainly and turned away to gape at the scenery. She sat down on the opposite end of the bench to rest her aching legs, the bear spray container tied around her waist making it uncomfortable to lean back. She looked down at Dace's waist.

"Don't you wear a gun?" she asked curiously.

"Usually. The holster is pretty heavy. I left it in the truck."

"What would you do if you encountered a bear?"

Dace turned a lazy eye on her. "Run." He chuckled at Kerrie's dry expression. "If I'm responding to a nuisance bear, I bring a sandbag shotgun. But I didn't think the black bear seen here two days ago would be a problem." He turned back to stare at the lake. "Besides, I'm off duty. My shifted ended an hour ago."

Kerrie stiffened, swinging her head to gape at him. "Off duty? Then what are you doing here?"

"I told you. I came up here to find you."

"Oh," Kerrie mumbled to her chagrin. Why couldn't she think of a more intelligent response?

"I hope you don't mind. I needed to stretch my legs anyway, and I appreciate the company."

Kerrie stared at the mountains surrounding them, her eyes fixed on a mystical waterfall cascading down one such peak. Dace was really putting her in a bad position. She had to work with Sandy, and she didn't want to create any animosity with her coworker. She opened her mouth to speak.

"What are you afraid of, Kerrie?" She turned to stare at him, but he remained relaxed, his eyes scanning the mountains. "I've seen it before, you know. The signs of abuse."

Kerrie gasped and grabbed her backpack in preparation for flight, her face burning.

Dace turned empathic gray eyes towards her and laid a restraining hand on her bag.

"Don't run off. It's actually not really safe to hike alone, even here." He shifted to face her, tracing a casual line with his finger along the grain of the log bench between them, apparently lost in thought.

Kerrie remained stiff. If she ran, he would likely chase her, the last thing she thought she could handle at the moment.

"I know you don't want to talk about it, and I should respect that, but..." He raised a sheepish face to hers. "I can't. I don't understand if it's the cop in me or what, but I have to know what happened to you." He gave her a crooked grin. "Let me ask you this. Are you safe at least?"

Kerrie looked away from the handsome face that broke down her reserve. She nodded. "I think so."

"Does he know where you are?"

Heart pounding, Kerrie stiffened again. His questions darkened her day and brought a frightening past to the beautiful serenity of the lake.

"I hope not."

She watched two deer emerge from the brush and approach the lake cautiously, pausing every few steps to search their surroundings, to assess the situation and listen for danger. She recognized the behavior. She'd lived with it for three years.

"Look," she pointed and whispered.

Dace turned to study the deer.

"They remind me of me—walking on eggshells, ears pricked for the slightest irregularity, eyes alert and wide open to catch a quick movement." Kerrie heard the words spilling from her lips, aware Dace returned his gaze to her face.

In a husky voice, he said, "I think I know what you mean. I've never been as powerless as you must have been, but I think I know the feeling."

Kerrie dragged her gaze from the beautiful russet deer, now drinking water from the lake. She met his forthright eyes before dropping hers to her clasped hands.

"Well, of course, you would. You've probably faced danger many times in your line of work."

He leaned forward abruptly and placed his knees on his elbows, with a quick glance at her and then back toward the lake. "I have run into a thug or two in addition to some unruly bears. But I chose my profession. I imagine it's quite likely you did not choose your brand of fear."

Kerrie shook her head. She certainly had not, but she had ignored the warning signs, and once she'd tasted the fury, she let it go too long. Her self-respect was in shreds.

She reached for her bag and rose, this time extending a hand to Dace. He took her hand and rose to his full height, towering above her. She blinked.

"He was tall, I take it," he said with a rueful smile.

Kerrie nodded. "He was tall...just like you." She turned to move away from him, but he laid a gentle finger on her arm. He stared down into her eyes.

"Not just like me," he said firmly. "I would never hurt you."

Kerrie's heart skipped a beat...more than one. She backed away and grinned to break the levity of the moment.

"I believe you, ranger. You're here to protect me from the big bad bear, remember." She stepped lightly over the pebbles and returned to the path.

Dace followed her with a smirk. "Okay, lil' missie. You lead the way. This time, I'll take up the rear and do the sightseeing."

Kerrie's cheeks flamed. "I beg your pardon," she sputtered as she moved out, hoping her shorts were long enough to cover her nether regions as she ascended the trail and wishing her backside were half as attractive as Dace's.

She hurried through the return climb, grateful when they finally reached the level part of the path. From there it would be either level or downhill. Her rear end would no longer be the prominent feature in his line of sight.

"Well, that was something," he murmured as they crested the final hill. Kerrie gasped for air, while Dace rested his hands on his hips and waited for her to catch her breath.

"What?" she panted as she bent over, keeping Dace to the front.

"The climb. What else?" he chuckled. "You don't think I meant anything improper, do you?" His deep laugh resounded in the forest. "I'm a gentleman, remember? The guy who tries to open doors for you?"

Kerrie tried to stifle the giggle that threatened to steal her precious air, but she failed and erupted into laughter. She straightened and clutched her aching ribs.

"I can't laugh. It hurts too much. Stop. Gentleman indeed!"

Dace held up two fingers. "Scout's honor. I stared at the back...of your hiking boots the whole way. No ma'am, not once did my eyes stray to your...uh...bottom. What kind of a guy do you take me for anyway?"

Kerrie shook her head.

"I have no idea. You are the most confusing man I think I've ever met." She prepared to resume the hike.

"Really? So you have given me some thought. All right!" Dace fell in behind her, much to her discomfort. The back of her neck tingled.

"No, I haven't, other than to appreciate the help with my truck and the good food." Kerrie stepped up the pace. "Aren't you forgetting someone?"

"Who?" Dace called from the rear, his footsteps quickening.

"Sandy," Kerrie said daringly.

"Sandy?"

"Yes, Sandy."

"Nope, I don't think I've forgotten her. At least I hope I haven't. Why? Did she say we had plans or something tonight?"

Kerrie paused momentarily, brought back to the reality of his unavailability. Her shoulders slumped. Dace almost ran into her, so suddenly did she stop.

"Hey there, I almost ran you over."

"No, I haven't seen Sandy since yesterday. She didn't say anything to me."

"Okay, good. I thought maybe I'd forgotten something. Well, come on, Speedy, lead the way."

Kerrie turned to head downhill, the beauty of the approaching waterfall and creek suddenly dimmed. She returned to the trailhead and the parking lot in silence, Dace close behind her.

"Well, thanks for everything, Dace. I'll see you at work."

"Good night, Kerrie. I'll see you soon."

She unhooked the bear spray to hand it to him, but he demurred.

"Keep it. I've got plenty."

She shrugged, climbed into the truck, and pulled out of the parking lot, keeping her eyes on his truck in the rearview mirror as he followed her down the road toward the West Entrance. He turned off into the housing area while she made her way out to the highway.

She stopped in a small town called Hungry Horse to get gas on her way back to town. When she got back into her truck, her cell phone rang.

"Hello?"

Silence.

Kerrie gripped the steering wheel. Oh please, no. It wasn't possible.

"Who is this? Stop calling me!" she shouted, and slammed the phone shut.

She pulled away from the pumps and into a parking space in front of the store. Grabbing her phone, she punched in a number. The phone rang.

"Hello."

Kerrie could have cried.

"Mom?" she couldn't hold back the whimper. "Mom?"

"Kerrie, honey, what is it?"

"I've been getting calls, but no one says anything. Did you call me?"

"No, honey. I haven't called you since the other day." Her mother hesitated. "Kerrie, do you think it's...Jack?"

Kerrie waited for a wave of nausea to pass before speaking. "Yes, I do. I don't know how he got the number, but I do. Who else could it be?"

"One of the other teachers from school? Someone from around here? It could be anyone, hon."

Kerrie dragged in a deep breath and then another. People walked in and out of the gas station convenience store, paying no heed to the woman in the small truck.

"Even if it was Jack, he still wouldn't know where you are. What area code are the calls coming in under?"

"They're showing *unknown caller.*"

"Oh." Her mother paused. "I thought you weren't going to answer the phone unless you knew who it was, Kerrie."

"I know, Mom, I wasn't. The first call caught me off guard in the night, and now...I just want to know...if it's him."

"Why, Kerrie? Why? You're not going to—"

"No, Mom. I'm not going to talk to him. I just need to know. It's like everything is starting all over again."

"Please don't talk to him, honey, please. Can you change your number?"

Kerrie sighed. "How many times do I have to do that, Mom?"

"Until he gives up, child. Until he leaves you alone."

"I'll think about it. I've just barely got this phone number memorized. I'll give it some thought. Maybe it wasn't him anyway."

"Probably not. I hope not," her mother added with emphasis.

"Well, I'd better get going. I'm sitting here in a gas station parking lot wearing out my welcome." Kerrie managed a chuckle. "I'll talk to you soon. I love you."

"I love you too, honey. Take care."

Kerrie closed the phone and stared at it for a moment before she stowed in back in her bag. She was overreacting. Jack couldn't possibly have gotten her number. Only her parents and the federal government had it. She backed the truck out the parking lot and got back on the highway. The federal government. Hmmm... She shook her head. Nah!

****

Dace climbed out of his truck and made his way into his apartment. Though the temperature seemed pleasant outside, he felt chilled and he wasn't quite sure why. He took off his clothes and threw them into the overly full laundry basket. A hot shower seemed just the ticket to warm him up. He stood beneath the steaming water and rested his forehead against the shower wall. Images of Kerrie materialized behind his closed eyes—her slender, petite legs, the curve of her spine as it moved down her back, the way sunlight bounced off her dark curls, the dancing light in her eyes as she teased him, the joyful sound of her rare laughter.

He wanted to be with her tonight, to spend more time in her company. Saying goodbye at the trailhead took all his willpower, but he had to let her go. She'd said goodbye in a flash, leaving him no time to suggest any other plans for the evening.

She seemed so vulnerable. It was all he could do not to take her into his arms and promise to take care of her forever. Dace reached up to rub his eyes. He doubted Kerrie would appreciate the gesture. It seemed clear she had a history of abuse, and he didn't want to take away whatever strength she'd finally found since she'd escaped.

He thought about her hiking alone and gritted his teeth. He grabbed the shampoo, dumped some in his hand, and began to scrub his hair vigorously. Foolish woman, he muttered silently. Stubborn. That's what she was. It wasn't safe to hike alone. He was going to have to keep a watchful eye on her. She would probably try it again.

He rinsed his head, wishing he could call her, but he dare not. Or could he?

Chapter Six

Kerrie arrived at work the next morning refreshed and ready to go, having turned off her phone the night before. She opted not to turn the phone on before she went to work. If her parents called, they would leave a message.

"Good morning," she sang out as she saw Sam outside the Park entrance.

"Well, good morning to you too, sunshine." He zipped his jacket up and rubbed his hands together. His breath came out in a frosty cloud. "I can't wait till it warms up in the mornings. It will by the end of June, I think."

"Oh really. I think it's great. Invigorating." She inhaled deeply. The air smelled crisp, the pine scent of the evergreen trees sharp and aromatic.

"I saw your truck at the Avalanche trailhead yesterday afternoon. Mary and I went up to the Loop and took a short hike out of there."

"Oh," Kerrie murmured. "Yeah, I did my first hike yesterday. All the way to Avalanche Lake." She grinned, knowing Sam and Mary would consider that a "beginner" hike.

"How'd you like it?" Sam opened the kiosk door for her as she took her drawer in to set up the register.

"Umm...good. It was great, in fact. Beautiful! A pretty easy hike for me."

"I saw Dace's SUV there. You probably ran into him then?"

"Umm..." Kerrie's heart skipped a beat and she pretended to immerse herself in opening procedures. Sam leaned on the window patiently. "What? Oh, Dace. Oh yeah, in fact, I did see him." She stared down the road, willing a car to come, then stared up the road to avoid eye contact. "Well, actually, he actually...uh...came with me to the lake." She nervously rubbed her nose. "I mean...I guess James was worried about me and sent him to check on me. Silly, really. I didn't have any bear spray and he brought me some. Silly, really."

Sam stared at her with a smirk on his face. "Really?"

Kerrie shuffled from side to side, leaning out the window to compel a car to come down the road toward her. No luck! She straightened and fidgeted with the cash register.

"Really. Silly. I'm fine. I'll be sure and take the bear spray next time. I hate to put anyone out."

Sam cocked his head, his grin widened. "Oh, I doubt you put Dace out. He's like that, you know? A nice guy. Likes to watch out for people."

"Really?" This time, Kerry asked the question. Her eyes flickered to Sam. "Well, he's a nice man."

"Yeah, he is," Sam agreed, his smile bright against his tanned and weathered face.

She swallowed hard. Time to dig. "James mentioned some sort of kidnapping story? Is that true?"

"Yup, true story. Guys fancied themselves mountain men, kidnapped a young gal in her teens and took her up into the mountains. The police needed someone familiar with the area and Dace led them in. They managed to ambush two of the guys and rescue the poor girl in time, cold but unharmed. Dace had to take off after the third desperado. Tackled him and brought him down." Sam shook his head and grinned from ear to ear. "Sure wish I could have been in on that."

Just then a car came through the gate and Kerrie turned to greet the visitors. She rubbed her arms to rid herself of the goose bumps that popped up at Sam's recounting of the tale. Dace grew taller and taller in stature as she learned more about him. Her hero worship had elevated him to the height of Paul Bunyan...at least. Not a good thing, she thought wryly, since tall men made her nervous.

"Well, I've got to get back to headquarters to pick up some stuff. See you later." Sam gave her a quick salute and moved away. Busy with the visitors, Kerrie nodded distractedly.

For the rest of the day, her heart raced every time a white SUV approached the gate. But to her disappointment, Dace never materialized. She wanted to ask if anyone in the office had seen him, but lacked the courage. It wouldn't do to inquire too much in Dace's whereabouts...especially if Sandy were in earshot.

She drove home slowly, out of sorts with herself and unsure of the reason. When she entered her apartment, she had a momentary vision of Suzie rushing up to her, tail wagging, barking in joy. But silence echoed in her small home away from home. Suzie had never been here.

She changed clothes slowly and headed to the bookstore, the walls of her apartment closing in on her.

"Hi, how are you?" Deenie asked as she steamed the milk for Kerrie's hot chocolate.

Kerrie threw a bright smile on her face.

"Good, good."

"How's it going at the Park?"

"Oh fine, getting busy now."

"I hope we get out there this year. I can't believe I live so close to the Park and hardly ever visit. What with school and the job, it's hard to find the time." Deenie gave Kerrie a mock pout.

"I can imagine. What are you studying?"

"Early childhood education. I'm going to be a teacher."

"Really? I'm a kindergarten teacher," Kerrie grinned.

"No kidding. Where do you teach? Are you just working at the Park for the summer? Your school year must end early. School doesn't get out until June around here." Deenie eyed her curiously.

Kerrie could have kicked herself. She'd spoken without thought. Her personal safety plan: give nothing away, open up to no one. Couldn't she even keep one lousy little secret?

She bit her lip and tap danced. "Oh, I used to teach. Not anymore. Yeah, I'm just working at the Park for the summer."

"Oh," Deenie mixed Kerrie's drink and handed the steaming cup to her. "Do you think you'll go back?"

"To teaching?" Kerrie shuffled from foot to foot. "Umm...maybe, someday. Not right now though."

"What's someday?" A deep voice spoke behind her, and Kerrie jumped, knocking over her drink.

"I'm sorry, I'm sorry," she gasped, as she grabbed a

wad of napkins and dabbed at the mess.

"Shoot, Kerrie, I'm sorry. I shouldn't have scared you like that. I know better." Dace leaned over the counter and grabbed a wet rag. He soaked up the liquid which spilled down the front of the counter.

"I've got a mop," Deenie appeared from behind the counter and began mopping.

Kerrie reached for the mop. "Let me. It's my fault."

"No, no, I'm good. This happens all the time. Go sit down. I'll bring you another one."

Dace finished cleaning and took the soaked napkins from Kerrie. "It's on me," he murmured. "I'm the one who scared you."

"Go away, shoo," Deenie paused and flicked her wrist. "It's on the house. Go sit down somewhere."

Dace put a hand behind Kerrie's back and guided her away from the coffee bar.

"Well, do you want to grab a seat?" He gestured toward a pair of easy chairs comfortably located near the magazines.

Kerrie nodded and dropped into one while Dace lowered himself into the other.

"I'm really sorry, Kerrie. I shouldn't have startled you like that. I think I knew I was going to make you jump, but I didn't realize how much."

"That's okay. I feel like an idiot. What a mess I made." Kerrie shook her head in dismay.

"I'm sure Deenie has seen worse." Dace glanced at her and then looked away, lightly tapping the armchair with his fingers. "You *do* have a well-developed startle response."

Kerrie, who had been studying her kneecaps, glanced up with heated cheeks.

"I act like a fruitcake, don't I? It's humiliating."

Dace leaned forward, his voice low. He placed a gentle hand on Kerrie's knee.

"It's normal, Kerrie. You should see the guys coming back from the war. We've had a few young veterans working in the Park."

"I haven't been in a war. It's stupid really...to be so jumpy. I wish I could control it."

"Well, you haven't told me much, but my guess is you

have been in a war...just a different battleground."

Kerrie's eyes blurred and she brushed a stray tear away with an impatient hand. She changed the subject.

"So, how was your day today? I didn't see you pass through the gate. Did you work?"

Dace cocked his head and stared at her for a moment. He nodded and leaned back in his chair. "Why, did you miss me?"

"Here you are." Deenie arrived, flourishing two drinks—coffee and a hot chocolate.

"Thank you, Deenie." Kerrie welcomed the interruption. So, the man wanted to flirt! She looked over her shoulder, wondering if Sandy would magically appear. Her eyes flickered toward him as he took his drink from Deenie. Just as soon as Dace climbed further up the pedestal Kerrie had created for him, he fell back down when he said things like, "Did you miss me?" Good men didn't flirt with other women when they were in stable relationships. At least, not in her book.

"So, you were saying?" Dace crossed his legs with an amused smile on his face.

"About what?"

"Ahhh. I see. You're forgetful," he nodded, the smile suspiciously resembling a smirk. "Something about missing me?"

Kerrie shook her head, her lips twitching. He was charming, if unavailable.

"Nope, I said no such thing. I merely mentioned that I did not see you today. You misunderstood."

Dace gave her a mock disappointed frown. "Perhaps I did. My apologies." His grin took her breath away. "I was in training today down in Kalispell. Can't ever have enough of that." His dry tone and raised eyebrows indicated a hint of mild sarcasm.

Kerrie toyed with her drink and grinned.

"Sam told me about that kidnapping two years ago and your role in it." She studied his face as she spoke.

He adjusted his legs and shrugged his shoulders. "Yeah, that was quite the hoot. The kidnappers really had no idea what they were doing. The older man, the father, wanted a girl for his sons, kind of like a wife. The dad and one son were fairly tame. But the other son, the one that got away...he was something else."

"How do you mean?"

"He was different...vicious. Planned the whole thing. I doubt the other two would have known what to do without him."

"So, you were the one who caught him."

"Yeah, took me half a day to track him down. Got the surprise of my life when I finally did find him."

"What?"

"A knife. A really big hunting knife. We thought we'd rounded up all the guns, but I didn't count on a knife."

"Really?"

Dace recrossed his legs and swallowed some coffee, eyeing her over the lid. He shrugged. "I don't know why I'm telling you this. It was a long time ago. They're all in prison now."

"What happened to the girl?"

"She returned to her family. Still drops me a Christmas card every year. Cute kid. I'm glad she recovered so well. I'd hate to think what would have happened..." A frown darkened his gray eyes.

"But it didn't. Because you rescued her." His ascent up the pedestal of worship advanced rapidly...as rapidly as her heartbeat when she gazed at him.

He gave her a startled look and then a lopsided grin, which failed to hide the bronzing of his cheeks. "Me and twenty other big guys in uniforms."

Kerrie laughed, a deep cleansing laugh that came from somewhere deep inside and wouldn't stop. With tears streaming down her face, she doubled over in her easy chair.

She wiped her eyes with the heel of her palms and saw Dace valiantly trying to contain his mirth behind a sputtering grin, but he failed and the deep, masculine sound of his laugh touched her in some long forgotten place. She couldn't remember the last time she'd heard a man laugh so freely...with such enjoyment. Jack's laugh...had always been at her expense.

One look at the moisture in his eyes brought forth another peel of laughter from her.

She pointed at him. "You're crying," she gasped. "A big guy like you and you're crying."

"Big guys cry too, missie. Don't let 'em fool you." He dashed a quick hand across his eyes and gulped for air.

"I know. I mean...I just...it's too funny." Another peal of laughter erupted and she clamped her hand over her mouth, virtually shutting off the sound. Kerrie's eyes darted around their immediate area, but no one seemed troubled by the noise.

"You'll fall off your pedestal if you're not careful," Kerrie teased in the hilarity of the moment.

"What pedestal?" Dace snorted, chuckles continuing to erupt.

"Oh, the pedestal I put you on." As soon as the words were out, Kerrie realized her mistake. What was she thinking?

"Pedestal, huh?" Dace tilted his head and grinned at her with mischief in his eyes. "So, how did I get on this pedestal?"

Kerrie caught her breath, desperately trying to come up with some plausible line to extricate herself from her accidental revelation.

"Oh, you know, big bad bear ranger and all. Any man in a uniform. Protector of the weak. Smokey the Bear." She gulped her hot chocolate as nonchalantly as she could, schooling her face into a playful grin that hardly represented her inner turmoil.

"Ahhh," he murmured, eyeing her over his coffee cup. "I see. You're teasing me."

"Yes, that's it, teasing you."

"By the way, Smokey the Bear is actually the National Forest Service's mascot."

"Oh, good gravy, really? How silly of me. I didn't know."

"So, I'm not really on a pedestal after all?"

"Oh, dear me, no. I was just kidding." Kerrie tried to look down the sliver of a hole in her cup lid to study her chocolate. She glanced up at his next comment.

"Too bad. That would have been nice. I'm not sure I could have stayed on it for long, but I would have been willing to try." Twinkling gray eyes boldly held her gaze. "Anything for a damsel in distress."

"You'd have to look further, Sir Knight. This damsel ain't in no distress." Kerry grinned.

"Uh oh, there's a sparkle in your eyes that tells me to tread lightly." Dace raised his eyebrows.

"Really? A sparkle in my eyes? How can you tell?"

"Because I've been watching you, Kerrie, and if I don't know anything else about you, I know that your gorgeous green eyes spit emerald sparks when you're mad, grow dark like a forest in a storm when you're troubled, and glow like jade when you're happy." He raised his cup and swallowed the last of his coffee. "How about some dinner?" He stood and held out a hand to a stunned Kerrie who obediently slipped her hand into his. He pulled her to her feet, but stepped back when she would have fallen into his arms.

"What are you in the mood for? How about Chinese?"

Kerrie nodded, suddenly mute and fighting a crazy desire to run to the bathroom to study her eyes. Did they really glow like jade? She snuck a quick glance at Dace's profile as she walked with him to the entrance. What an enigma! She had never...in her life...heard a man describe her eyes in such a manner...or for that matter, any part of her body. And he really shouldn't have been talking to her in such a way. He obviously liked women, unfortunately for Sandy. Kerrie couldn't help herself. She felt certain Sandy wouldn't approve of his...attentions, but Kerrie couldn't stay away from him. And she wanted to climb right up on his pedestal and rest at his feet, casting the occasional adoring glance at his face as he stood with arms akimbo...protecting the world from unruly bears.

"Kerrie?" Dace held the passenger door of his truck open. A sense of shame washed over her and she hesitated. She held back and dropped her head, staring at her toes as she stepped from side to side.

"I'm sorry, Dace. I can't go. I-I don't think it's a good idea." She turned away to head for her own truck.

"Kerrie, wait! What happe—"

Dace grabbed her arm, lightly—but all grabs were suspect in her world.

She batted at his hand. "Take your hands off me," she shrieked. She backed up rapidly. "Don't you dare touch me." She flung away from him and dashed to her own truck, barely aware of her actions. She jumped in and peeled out of the parking lot, tears streaming unchecked down her face, lips chattering, body quivering.

She took one look in the rearview mirror and satisfied herself that he remained in the parking lot, staring after her. Then she carefully made her way out of the downtown area and pulled into her apartment building parking lot without mishap. Tears continued to blur her vision. She knew she shouldn't have driven, but her primal instinct to flee had overcome free will. Safely out of harm's way, she clearly remembered the shock and alarm on Dace's face as she raged like a shrew. He must have thought she'd lost her mind. She lowered her forehead to the steering wheel and cried, wracked by sobs that seemed to have no end.

Kerrie knew what had happened. When Dace grabbed her arm, she'd been instantly transported back in time, and it was once again Jack grabbing her arm...leaving bruises. Her instinct for survival took over, banishing all rational thought, and she fled.

Would she ever be normal again? Able to interact with other people...men...without falling apart?

She shuddered and wiped her face with the back of her hands. She made her way into her apartment and threw herself on the bed face down. Her tears had dried. She curled into a ball, and stared at the darkening sky outside her window. Stress and exhaustion took their toll and she fell asleep.

The incessant ringing of her cell phone awakened her. With half closed eyes, she searched the bed for the purse she'd tossed down and found the phone. She opened it, remembering her mother's cautions. *Unknown caller.*

Kerrie stared at the phone groggily. The ring continued. She opened it.

"Hello."

There was no answer.

"Hello, who is this?"

"Hello, Kerrie. Did I wake you? It must be late where you are."

Chapter Seven

"Jack." Kerrie swallowed hard and sat up, searching the darkened room as if he were there. "How did you get my number? What do you want?"

"I got your number, Kerrie, because I wanted it, and you know I usually get what I want."

A shiver ran up Kerrie's spine, and she drew her knees up and huddled against the headboard, pulling the comforter around her.

"Not this time. I'm gone. You'll never find me."

"If I found your number, how long do you think it will be before I find you? What makes you think I don't already know where you are?"

Kerrie remembered his first words. *It must be late where you are.* Had he found her? How? She'd been so careful.

"What do you want?"

"I just want to talk to you, Kerrie. I miss you."

"Well, I don't miss you, and I don't want to talk to you. It's over. Finally."

"Kerrie. Please don't say it like that. Don't throw all our years away. We can still make this work. Please come back to me."

Kerrie stiffened and swallowed the bile that rose to her throat.

"Are you serious?"

"Yes, I am. I love you. I've changed. Things are going to be different now...even if you don't come back to me. I've changed. I just want you to know that. I'm seeing a counselor now. He's helped me understand my temper, taught me some coping mechanisms."

Kerrie heard his words, but she didn't want to listen to them. Nothing would make her return to him. Nothing.

"Kerrie?"

"What?"

"Are you listening to me?"

"I heard you, but it's too late. I don't care how much you change. I'm never coming back."

"You've got to come home sometime. I know your parents miss you."

"What would you know about it? They hate you, by the way."

"I know, Kerrie, and they have every right to. What I did was horrendous. Unforgivable. I'm sorry I hurt you."

"Which time, Jack?" Distance gave her a courage she never had in his presence.

"Kerrie, I'm in a twelve-step recovery program for batterers. I have to make amends to the people I've hurt. I hurt you the most, and I'm sorry for every time I laid a hand on you. I had no right."

"No, you didn't." His abject apologies only inflated her righteousness. She didn't care what kind of program he was in.

"Okay, Kerrie. Okay. I hear you." He hesitated and then continued in a husky voice. "I still love you, Kerrie. I'll always love you."

Kerrie closed her eyes, a single hot tear squeezed out and rolled down her cheek. She couldn't help but remember the loving man she thought she'd known many years ago.

"It's too late, Jack. I have to go. Please don't call again."

"Ker—" She closed the phone, certain he would not call again. Hopefully, his therapist would tell him to move on. A recovery program for batterers. She hoped for his sake that it would be effective. She would never know.

She slid off the bed and shuffled into the bathroom to wash her face. When she returned, her phone began to ring again. She stared at it. *D. Mitchell.* A Montana area code. Who could that be?

"Hello," she answered in a cautious voice.

"Kerrie?" Dace's hesitant tone made her cringe with shame.

"Dace."

"How are you?"

"Good."

"I'm sorry I grabbed your arm. I had no right to do that."

"Oh, Dace. I feel like such an idiot. I'm sorry I overreacted. It was terribly rude."

"No, no. Not at all." He hesitated. "Are you all right?"

"Sure, I'm fine."

"Did something happen?" His words seemed measured. "I thought we were going to dinner and then..."

Kerrie drew in a deep breath. "I-I..."

"Listen, you are well within your rights to say no. Honestly. I certainly wouldn't push you. I just thought..." His voice trailed off.

How could she explain? What words would she use? *Dace, I think you're a great guy...the best, in fact...but I'll bet Sandy thinks so too.*

"Dace, I-I..." Words failed her.

"I understand, Kerrie. I understand." His tone quickened. "Well, listen, I'd better get off the phone and get back to what I was doing. I really just called to apologize for manhandling you. I'll see you at work, okay?"

"No need—" The line went dead. Kerrie bit her lip and stared at the little phone which brought her such heartache. Stupid phone! She flung it across the room, watching it land on the carpeting near the bathroom door, half of her wishing it broke, the other half hoping it hadn't.

Well, she'd told him, hadn't she? Or had she? Kerrie replayed the conversation in her mind. Not once had she mentioned Sandy to him. Not once had she made any effort to discover why he thought he could dine with other women when he had a girlfriend.

She jumped off the bed restlessly and tossed her clothes aside to step into the bathroom and a hot shower. A short while later, calm and relaxed, she climbed into bed vowing to swear off men forever...or reaffirming her previous vow to swear off men forever. At long last, Jack was out of her life. As for Dace, she needed to forget about him and focus on enjoying her short season at the Park.

****

Dace lay back on his bed and stared at the phone in his hand. He fought a burning desire to throw it against the wall, knowing all he would have left was a broken phone. No Kerrie.

He cursed himself and rose from the bed to pace around the small apartment. How could he have been so wrong? Was he so pathetic that he saw interest in her eyes where there was none? Even given Kerrie's history of being abused, her actions made no sense. Why did she say she would go to dinner and then change her mind? She said, "I don't think this is a good idea." What wasn't a good idea?

He picked up the phone again to stare at her number, the number he got from work. He knew then when he wrote her number down that he'd pay the piper for breaking the rules. It was out of line. He shouldn't have done it.

Still, she hadn't seemed angry when he called. A bit confused, hesitant. Maybe sorry for him?

Dace banged his hand against his head. Oh, man, she was probably trying to let him off lightly. How had he missed the signals? She wasn't interested in him. But she had no idea how to tell him.

Dace stepped into the bathroom, planted his hands on the counter and stared at his reflection.

"You idiot! All this time, she's been trying to tell you she's not interested. It doesn't matter why. Maybe she's scared. Maybe she doesn't want to be around men. Who could blame her? And maybe, big boy, you're just not her type." Dace narrowed his eyes as he lectured his alter ego.

"What a fool! You're no better than that stalking ex-lover of hers. You kept pushing and pushing until she didn't know what to do."

Dace straightened up and pulled his shoulders back.

"Let her go. Just let her go." With a final nod, he strode briskly out of the bathroom and threw himself onto the bed, putting the pillow over his head and biting down hard.

Chapter Eight

In the weeks that followed, Kerrie's heart ached a little more each day as Dace drove through the West Entrance with a brief wave in her direction but little else in the way of recognition. She found no chance to speak to him privately, and in truth, did not seek him out. What could she say?

He stopped by the West Entrance occasionally to pick Sandy up, presumably for lunch, but he did not seek Kerrie out in the kiosk. And why should he?

Visitor attendance during the height of the season increased threefold, and cars lined up outside the Park to pay their entrance fees. The hectic days took their toll, and Kerrie simply poured herself into bed when she got home, too tired to find her way to the bookstore. She'd gone to her favorite haunt only once following her repudiation of Dace in the parking lot, but the magic vanished from her sanctuary and the bookstore became a lonely and empty building full of cold, lifeless books.

She studied Glacier National Park trail maps at home and on her days off, she ventured out on several small day hikes, careful to stow the bear spray in her backpack. On the first such hike to a place called Apgar Overlook, she found herself stopping often, holding her breath, searching the path behind her. But it wasn't the sound of a bear she listened for. She couldn't shake the feeling...or the wish...that somehow Dace would materialize as he had before. He never did.

"How's it going this morning, Kerrie?"

Kerrie waved a visitor through and turned to look at Sam's weathered face. Bright blue eyes flashed between tanned Paul Newman crinkles.

"Good, Sam. It's a little bit slower this morning than it has been. The break is nice."

He leaned against the kiosk keeping one eye on the road for approaching traffic.

"Yeah, happens once in a while. Visitors keep coming and coming, and then all of a sudden one day, everybody decides to stay home...kinda like they called each other on a telephone tree." His lips twitched. He turned to meet her eyes. "It's your Friday, isn't it?"

Kerrie nodded with a grin. "Sure is. It's great having a Friday on a Monday. No more Monday morning blues for me."

"What did you do that you had the Monday morning blues? Sounds like a 9 to 5 job to me."

"Oh, I used to teach kindergarten. It was so hard to drag myself out of bed some mornings, especially in the winter."

"A school teacher? I don't think I knew that. Where did you teach?"

Kerrie realized her mistake. A car approached and she turned away to greet the visitors with a fixed smile on her face, wondering how she could discretely guide the conversation away from her past. Maybe Sam would lose interest and leave while she took money and made change.

She stalled as long as possible, but Sam remained fixed in place leaning against the window of the kiosk. She fiddled with brochures and fidgeted with pens and pencils, hoping another vehicle would quickly approach, but there seemed to be another lull in traffic. She changed the subject.

"Sam, I'm thinking of taking an overnight hike to Sperry Chalet this weekend. It'll be my first. What do you think?"

Sam adjusted his perfectly balanced hat and shifted from one foot to the other.

"Who's going with you?"

"Ummm...no one. I thought I'd try it on my own." Kerrie could have predicted Sam's response, but the question served to divert him from her past and solicit useful information from an experienced park ranger and hiker.

"That's not a good idea." Her heart sank at Sam's blunt comment, but she forged ahead.

"Well, I know it's not ideal, but I don't really know anyone else." Too pathetic. "That is, I don't know anyone who has the same days off as I do, so..." Good gravy, was she wheedling? "So, I thought..."

Sam shook his head firmly. "It's not a good idea, Kerrie. Are you sure there's no one else who can hike with you? I'd ask Mary, but she works tomorrow and the next day."

"Oh, thanks, Sam. That's nice of you. No, I don't know anyone else, but I'll be fine. It's just seven miles to the chalet. I'll spend the night there and hike back. Everyone does it. I'll be fine."

Just then, Sandy opened the door of the office.

"Sam, phone call." Sandy gave Kerrie a quick wave while she waggled the phone in Sam's direction.

"All right, coming," he called over his shoulder as he raised an admonishing finger in Kerrie's direction.

"I really wish you'd rethink this, Kerrie. Even Mary never hikes alone."

Kerrie thankfully turned toward an approaching car, hoping Sam would soon forget the conversation. She could have kicked herself. In an effort to divert his attention from her past, she'd raised a subject that he'd taken issue with.

Her shift passed slowly, and she was thankful when Sandy replaced her.

"Sam says you're hiking up to Sperry Chalet by yourself tomorrow. Is that true?" Sandy slipped her cash drawer in and scanned the road for oncoming traffic before turning to face Kerrie who paused at the entrance.

"Yeah," she mumbled sheepishly. "I take it you don't approve either."

"Not really, but I'm not much of a hiker. Kayaking is more my thing. I usually go out with a group every weekend, either on the river or on the lake."

"Sounds wonderful."

"Yeah, it is." She eyed Kerrie pensively. "So you don't know anyone around to hike with tomorrow?"

With a quick shake of her head, Kerrie raised her chin. "No, you know I haven't been here long. But as I told Sam, it's a popular hike and I'm sure there will be plenty of people along the way. Besides, I've got my trusty bear spray." Kerrie grinned, until she remembered it was Sandy's man, Dace, who had given her the spray. She gulped and lowered her eyes.

"Glad to hear it." Sandy turned toward an approaching vehicle. "Well, have a good time. Let me know how it goes. I'll see you in a couple of days."

Kerrie made good her escape that evening without any further conversations with Sam on the subject of her proposed hike the following day. Sandy wished her well again, but didn't raise any further concerns. As she drove home, Kerrie wondered if Dace made up one of Sandy's kayaking party.

Upon entering her empty apartment, she experienced a pang of loneliness, exaggerated by the admonitions not to hike alone which served as a reminder that she was indeed on her own. When her phone rang, she pounced on it gratefully.

"Hello?" *Mom? Dace?*

"Kerrie? It's me."

Kerrie caught her breath and stared at the phone. *Unknown number.* How could she have been so stupid again?

"What is it, Jack? I thought we agreed you wouldn't call again." Her heart pounded and she fought to keep her voice steady.

"I didn't agree to that. I couldn't bear it if I couldn't ever talk to you again."

The sincerity in his voice tugged at her heart. How many times had she fallen for his charm, for the little boy lost routine that may or may not have been authentic? Too many. She steeled herself against him, against memories of a love gone wrong.

"Jack. It's over. I'm gone. You'll never find me...thankfully. Move on. Please. I'm glad to know that you're in therapy. That will be very helpful for the next woman you fall in love with. There has to be another woman...because it isn't going to be me. Please don't call me anymore." This time, she waited for his assurance.

"Kerrie, I love you. I will find you. I have to. We need to be together. I need to be with you."

Kerrie's stomach heaved. Time and distance blocked the power those words once held over her. Only nausea and a desire to flee remained.

"Jack, don't call me again. Don't try to find me. You

never will. Goodbye." Kerrie snapped her phone shut and dropped it on the couch, uncaring if it fell into a crevice, never to resurface again.

Unwilling to touch the offending instrument even to call her mother for support, she grabbed her purse, threw a jacket over her uniform and ran out the door, desperate to get away from Jack...from the sound of his voice.

She jumped into her truck and headed to the bookstore—the only place she could think of at short notice. Though she didn't really want to be around other people, she thought she would just slide into a comfortable seat and hide behind a book. As much as she didn't want to socialize, she didn't want to be alone...with her fears.

Kerrie gripped the steering wheel with moist palms. Jack couldn't find her, could he? Could he? How had he gotten her phone number? Could he find her location just as easily? She hoped not. As she sped toward the lights of the town, Kerrie kept a watchful eye on her rearview mirror. But no headlights appeared behind her, no one followed.

She pulled into the bookstore parking lot and jumped out of the truck with a harried glance at the surrounding cars. Jack drove a small red sports car. There was no small red sports car in the parking lot. Sprinting into the store, she paused just inside the door to collect herself. The overhead bright lights and hum of people's voices grounded her in reality, bringing a measure of relief. Jack couldn't possibly know where she was. He would not *find* her. She must change her phone number.

Kerrie bypassed the café area and made her way to a secluded easy chair near the magazines, grabbing a large coffee table pictorial book on Europe along the way. She sank into a seat and pulled the book up toward her face, resting the heavy volume on one arm of the chair as she hid behind it.

She sighed, allowing the tension to ease from her neck. Her shoulders slumped as she stared at a page depicting a panoramic view of Paris from the Eiffel Tower. She would love to be in Paris at the moment, but she didn't have a passport. If she had planned her escape from Jack better...

"Kerrie."

A familiar voice interrupted her newly found sense of security. She raised startled eyes to find Dace standing above her.

"Don't tower over me, for Pete's sake." To her consternation, she snipped at him.

His eyes narrowed and his chin hardened before he turned to move away. She dropped the oversized volume in her lap.

"Dace, I'm sorry. I-I...I'm sorry. Wait."

Dace paused and turned back to face her, an unreadable expression in his eyes.

"I didn't mean to be so rude. I-I have trouble with people standing over me...that's all."

He tilted his head to the side as if he could understand her better with a skewed view. She couldn't help but grin at her irreverent thoughts, and she tilted her head to match his.

A slow grin spread across his face, and he shook his head slightly. Kerrie noticed with relief that he did not approach her again, but slid into a nearby seat.

"I don't know what I'm going to do about you, Kerrie." A rueful smile played on his lips, and her heart rolled over in her chest.

"I'm a bit neurotic, I guess."

"I remember." His eyes widened. "Not that you're neurotic, but that you have reason to be." Dace gave himself a playful smack to the forehead. "I've got to learn to tread lightly around you, I think."

Kerrie eyed him suspiciously. Sometimes, she just didn't understand him.

"You don't have to tread any which way with me, Dace. I don't really see you that much."

He gave her a sideways look, one eyebrow slightly raised. "You don't, huh? Did you miss me?"

"What!" Bright red color flooded Kerrie's face. She could feel the heat. "What are you talking about?" She narrowed her eyes against his perceived smirk, though in truth she knew he was just teasing.

"Relax, Kerrie. I'm just playing with you. I just thought when you said you hadn't seen me that much..." He let his sentence trail off and eased out a mock heavy sigh.

"Oh, that. I don't know why I said that." There was no backpedaling available. She gave up and stared down at the book in her lap.

"How have you been? It *has* been a long time since we talked, hasn't it?"

"Has it?" She fidgeted with the corner of the book, keeping her eyes fixed on the cover while waiting for the color in her cheeks to recede.

"Yes, it has. Is everything all right? You seem a bit jumpy."

"Do I?" The other corner of the book took a beating.

"Stop fiddling with that book."

She obeyed and raised startled eyes in his direction. He leaned forward now, elbows resting on hips.

"Is everything okay? You're still in your uniform."

Her eyes traveled down to her dark green slacks. The phone call. Jack.

"I forgot to change," she shrugged carelessly.

"Kerrie." His tone was resolute, determined. "Stop hedging. I think you need someone to talk to. And even if you don't, I need to hear your story. *I* need to." Blue-gray eyes locked on her face, refusing to allow her to look away.

"I don't want to talk about it, Dace. I don't think I can." Her voice was hushed, almost a whisper.

"Try." He glanced over his shoulder. "There's no one around. I'm worried about you, and I'd like to know why I'm worried." He gave her a lopsided grin, eliciting a small smile from her.

Kerrie chewed on her lip, a sense of dread weighing heavily on her chest.

"Dace, every time I think about it or try to talk about it, I feel slightly sick. I feel it now." She rubbed goose bumps from her arms.

"How about if I ask you questions? Would that help?"

"Kind of like a police interview?" A corner of her mouth twitched.

"Yeah, something like that. If the shoe fits..." He grinned.

"Okay."

"Okay." Dace nodded decisively and sat back in his chair. "Ummm..." He seemed suddenly at a loss for words as he looked at her and down at his clasped hands, thumbs rotating back and forth.

"That's not a very good beginning."

"No, it isn't, is it? A lot harder than I thought." He gave her a sheepish grin. He sat forward. She brought the heavy volume up to her chest and hugged it.

"Are you hiding from a stalker?"

Kerrie gasped at the directness of the question. She nodded dumbly, unable to mouth words.

Dace's eyes softened. He reached a hand and touched her arm briefly before reclasping his hands as he leaned against his legs.

"Your husband?"

Kerrie shook her head. She wished she could help, but her jaw seemed locked.

"A boyfriend, significant other?"

Kerrie took a deep breath and nodded.

"Does he know where you are?"

She gritted her teeth, grimaced and shook her head.

Dace surveyed her through narrowed eyes. "You don't seem certain about that. What's going on? Is he here? In town?"

Kerrie shook her head and took another deep breath.

"He called me."

"So he has your number."

"He does now."

"So you need to change your phone number."

She nodded, embarrassed she hadn't done so after the first phone call.

"How did he get your number? Did someone you know give it to him?"

Kerrie shook her head. "My mom and dad are the only one's who have it...and the Park. He couldn't have gotten it from either place...at least I don't think so."

"I'll make some inquiries at work. It *is* on the employee listing, but that's for official use. Although I didn't use it for official use, did I?" He tightened his lips and shook his head.

"That's okay."

"Not really, probably frightened you getting a call from a stranger."

She remained mute.

"Do you have a restraining order against him?"

Kerrie nodded. "In Washington."

"Is that where you're from? I'm not sure that's valid in Montana. You might need to get another one. I'll look into it."

"Yes, from eastern Washington. A small town you've probably never heard of."

"What has he said when he called?"

Kerrie swallowed hard. "Just that he still loves me and can't let me go." She gave Dace a direct look. "He knows it's over. I've told him. I left without a word, gave up my life, my friends, my dog."

Dace shook his head, his brows drawn together in a frown.

"I'm sorry, Kerrie. How long did you live with him?"

"Five years."

"How long did he...did he...was he abusive the entire time?"

"No, not for the first two years. It didn't start until the third year. I suppose you wonder why I didn't leave before." She had no excuse. What could she say?

"No, not really. I've heard many stories. I know it's not easy to leave. Let me guess. Did he say he was sorry and promise to change?"

"Every time," she mumbled with downcast eyes. "Every time."

He touched her arm again briefly. "Kerrie, it's easy to believe that people we love...who love us...will change. Sometimes they just can't."

Her eyes flew to his.

"Don't be too hard on yourself. You gave him three years to change, but you finally got out." He paused for a moment. "Was it bad?"

Kerrie looked away from his sympathetic gaze. "Sometimes. Then months would pass before something would happen again." She rested her chin on the book against her chest. "But no matter how sorry he was, he would do it again."

"Temper?"

Kerrie nodded. "He just couldn't stand to be crossed. His self-esteem was...is...so fragile that he couldn't seem to tolerate it when I disagreed." Kerry shook her head. "It doesn't matter why really. It took me three years to realize that I wasn't causing the violence, that no matter what, he had no right to hit me or choke me or kick me."

A hiss escaped Dace's lips. She looked at him. A muscle twitched in his tightened jaw. The knuckles of his clasped hands shone white against his tan.

"Did you ever call the police?"

Kerrie shook her head. "No. I probably should have gone to the hospital a few times, but I didn't." She hung her head. "No, I never went to the police...not until I finally got the restraining order."

Dace leaned in to peer under her lowered lashes. "You blame yourself."

She raised trouble eyes to search his face. "I do. I never should have let it go on for so long, and I should have gone to the police. I-I just couldn't bear to see him go to jail."

"I understand."

"At any rate, he says he's in counseling now, so maybe he'll change."

Kerrie realized what she'd said when Dace stiffened. "You're not...thinking about—"

She raised a hand. "No, no, oh no. Never." She shook her head and eyed him squarely. "Never."

Dace's sigh of relief spoke volumes. "Well, I'm glad to hear that."

Kerrie gave him a rueful grin. "No, I'm just glad he's getting help. But he's in my past...and that's where I hope he stays."

"Good to hear, Kerrie."

Kerrie glanced up at him curiously. "You seem to know quite a bit about domestic violence. Why is that?"

Dace leaned back in his chair. "Oh you know, legal aid stuff...Baltimore, although that sort of thing goes on every in every socioeconomic class...as you well know."

Kerrie nodded but her ears burned. "Legal aid?"

Dace nodded, his eyes straying to a distant spot to his left.

"And?"

"Yes?" He returned his gaze to her inquisitive face, his lips twitching.

"Legal aid?"

"I worked as a low-paid lawyer for legal aid for a while."

Kerrie sat back in her chair and studied him with rounded eyes. Would the man never cease to surprise her?

"An attorney?"

"Yup."

Kerrie wasn't about to let him clam up on her.

"Well, tell me, why did you leave? Why are you working for the Park Service? Surely this job pays a lot less?"

He grinned. "Well, the pay isn't too much lower than that of a legal aid attorney to tell you the truth...but I left because I didn't like being cooped up indoors, and I wanted to travel. I just couldn't sit still." He gestured expansively. "Hence, the Park Service, the great outdoors, lots of different parks."

Kerrie put her book down on her lap and rested her clasped hands over it, completely involved in ferreting out Dace's past.

"Just like that?" she asked disbelievingly.

"Just like that. I lawyered for about ten years before I decided to give it up. Had the craziest idea to join the Park Service and here I am, some ten years later...enjoying myself."

"Are you?" Kerrie wasn't quite convinced. She thought she saw something in his eyes at times, a sort of wistfulness. She shook her head at her whimsical thoughts.

"You bet." His response was firm, his blue-gray eyes facing her squarely.

"So, you're about what? Forty-four or so?"

He raised his brows and eyed her carefully.

"Good guess."

"No marriage or family in all those years?" Kerrie knew she was treading on slippery rocks, but she had to press the issue. What was behind the look in his eyes? Perhaps he would talk about Sandy now. Were they engaged? She watched him shift position in his seat.

"Nope, no marriage, no family. I came close once, but she didn't want to take off to the wilderness with me. And I couldn't stay." His lopsided grin caught at her heart. Or perhaps it was the lack of matching laughter in his eyes.

Kerrie jumped in with both feet. She had to know. "What about Sandy?" She dropped her eyes and held her breath, cringing as she waited for his response.

"Sandy? She just started in the Park Service about five years ago. She likes to travel as much as I do."

She raised her eyes to study his angular and tanned face. His eyes glowed as he discussed Sandy. Even white teeth grinned at Kerrie. His noncommittal expression gave no additional information. He hadn't given her the complete answer she wanted, but she couldn't pry any further. At least not now. Questions nipped at the edge of her tongue, and she clamped her mouth shut on them. After all, she actually enjoyed her ignorance and denial of their relationship. It allowed her fantasies about him to take flight without too much of a headwind.

Her face reddened on the last thought and she raised a covering hand to her cheek.

He leaned forward. "Are you all right? You look flushed." He ran his fingers along her hand with a feather light touch.

Kerrie stiffened and backed away quickly, an instinctive reaction she had come to hate.

Dace pulled his hand back and sat back in the chair.

"I'm sorry," Kerrie rushed in. "I'm sorry. It's not personal. I do the same thing to my mother when she touches my face. I'm sorry." She pulled the book protectively up to her chest again.

Dace leaned forward again but did not touch her this time. "Don't be, honey. Don't be. I understand. I shouldn't have touched you."

"No, I don't want people to avoid... I mean, I want people to touch...that is, I don't want to be a freak." She lowered her chin on the massive volume and stared down at the ground. She couldn't deny that she craved Dace's touch. Had he just called her honey?

"I know you don't. You're not a freak. Just gun shy...that's all." Dace grinned kindly at her, weakening her guard, bringing her dangerously near to tears. She changed the subject.

"So, how's the bear business?" She brought a determined smile to her face.

"Good. The bears have been busy. It's huckleberry

season, you know...and they love their huckleberries."

"Have the poor creatures had any run ins with the law lately?" Her smile widened.

Blue-gray eyes twinkled. "A few. We've closed off a few trails due to grizzly activity."

Kerrie stiffened. "Not the trail to Sperry Chalet?"

Dace's eyes narrowed and he searched her face. Kerri bit her unruly lip.

"No, that's still open," he responded. "Why do you ask? Are you planning a hike up there?"

Kerrie would never understand why she gave the answer she did.

"No, no. I just... Well, some visitors at the gate were planning on hiking up tomorrow. They asked if it was safe. I told them I hadn't heard anything." Kerrie forced a casual shrug while her eyes scanned the bookstore in an effort to avoid his direct gaze.

"Oh. Well, no, I haven't heard anything. You had me worried there for a moment. I thought you were going to try one of those "I'm going by myself" hikes."

Her lying eyes flickered at him uncertainly, and she looked away again. "Me? Oh, no, too far for me. I might some day though," she murmured.

"Well, plan ahead and find a hiking companion. Don't go alone." He wagged what she considered an irritating finger, and her spine stiffened. She unfolded her legs and lowered the book.

"Well, Dace, I've got to get going. As you can see, I haven't even gotten out of my uniform. I think I'll head home and make it an early night."

She rose and Dace stood up beside her. She leaned down to put the book on the table next to her chair, letting her hair sweep forward to cover her face. Remorse and guilt engulfed her...and loneliness. She turned to Dace.

"Thanks for being such a good listener, Dace. I feel better for having talked to you."

Dace held out a hand palm up, inviting her to place her hand in his. She laid her hand in his trustingly. He did not close his fingers over hers and she was thankful for the chance to pull her hand away if she needed.

"You're welcome. Talk to me anytime. Call me

anytime. Do you still have my number from when I called?"

Kerrie nodded mutely.

"I mean it. Call me anytime...if something happens...if he calls you again...or even if you need a hiking buddy."

Kerrie pulled her guilty hand from his. "Thanks, Dace. I will." She lied with a heavy heart. The man had a life of his own. The last thing anyone needed was a clingy "victim."

Kerrie turned away and headed for the door and the loneliness of the dark night. With her head bowed low, she made her way to her truck and dragged herself into the driver's seat.

Intent on trying to understand why Sandy had Dace and she did not, Kerrie didn't register headlights in her rearview mirror for about a mile. She thought nothing of it, other than wishing it were Dace following her home with an insistence that he was in love with her and wanted to stay the night. Thankful no one could see her reddened face in the dark, she made a left toward her street. The lights followed.

Kerrie's palms began to sweat and she straightened in her seat, staring at the lights behind her while trying to keep an eye on the road ahead. Dace had a large truck. Though she couldn't see the vehicle in the darkness, it seemed smaller than a truck, the headlights lower to the ground. Kerrie didn't know whether to speed up or slow down.

She made the first right turn available, three blocks before her street. She wasn't about to lead someone to her apartment building. She caught her breath and held it. The vehicle followed.

Chapter Nine

Anxiety gripped Kerrie's consciousness. Her hands shook on the steering wheel. She spied a well-lit house and pulled into the double driveway next to a large SUV. She turned off her engine and lights and waited with a pounding heart. In her rearview mirror, she could see the car, a white sports model, drive slowly past the house. She turned to follow its progress down the road. Brake lights flashed as the car came to a stop in the middle of the road just past the house. Kerrie ducked down into her seat, hugging herself to stop the shaking, biting down hard to ease her chattering teeth. She peeked up over the edge of the side panel and watched as the brake lights dimmed and the car resumed its slow progress down the road. The driver paused at the corner, then made a left hand turn. She kept a watchful eye on it as long as possible until it disappeared from sight.

Kerrie slowly straightened in her seat and glanced at the house in front, vaguely wondering why no one opened the front door to discover who parked in their driveway. She waited for five minutes, keeping a vigilant eye on the road behind, knowing it would be easier to explain her presence in the driveway than to deal with an unknown car following her home.

The first name that came to mind was Jack. What if it were Jack? He had followed her before, when they still lived together. She'd gone to the library one night...just to get out of the house...and he had followed her. She remembered the argument that followed, his accusations of infidelity, the painful and abrupt end to her words as his hand ran across her face. She'd gone to the library a week after that and he had followed, but she learned not to argue. He just wanted to make sure her real destination was, in fact, the library.

With a wary final search of the empty streets, she started the engine and backed out of the driveway, pausing in the street to see if any headlights materialized in the darkness. Nothing. She made her way home slowly and cautiously, anxious eyes scanning the length of every street. The parking lot of her apartment complex was full, but no white sports car lurked in a hidden spot. She parked and ran up the stairs, shaking hands fumbling with the key while she cast harried glances over both shoulders.

She pushed into her apartment, locking the door behind her. Throwing on all the lights, she sank onto the couch and grabbed her cell phone. She would have loved to call Dace and beg him to baby sit her, but she called her mother.

"Hello."

"Hi, Mom." Kerrie could not keep the anxiety from her voice.

"Honey, what's wrong?"

"I'm scared, Mom. I'm just scared. I think I was followed home tonight."

"What? In a small town like that? I thought you were safe there. What's going on?"

"It was a white sports car. Jack had a sports car. What if he got a new car?"

"Oh honey, it couldn't have been Jack."

"Why not?" Kerrie's voice squeaked.

"Well, because I saw him yesterday...in his red sports car. I saw him at the mall. I doubt if he drove all the way over there and suddenly switched the color of his car."

"Really? You saw him?"

"Yes, and I ignored him. He tried to talk to me, but I shook my head and walked on. I hate the man, Kerrie. I just hate him."

Kerrie's lips twitched. "Thanks, Mom. I wish I could hate him, but I feel too much guilt. It's nice to just hear some unadulterated hate."

Her mom chuckled. "So, did someone follow you all the way home?"

Kerrie sank back into her couch and pulled her feet up. "Oh, geez, Mom. I probably overreacted. Good gravy. A car drove down the street behind me, and I panicked and assumed it was Jack."

"Well, I doubt if it was. So, if it wasn't Jack, was it

someone else?"

"I doubt it, Mom. It was probably just some car going in the same direction. I'm just slap happy I guess."

"That's an apt term," her mother said dryly.

"Bad choice of words, Mom. I'd rather not remember."

"I know, honey. Is everything else okay? Have you made any friends there?"

"Ummm...yeah, some, Mom."

"Good. You need a social life. You need support from friends. Does anyone know...about...you know..."

"I told one person. Well, he figured it out. He's in law enforcement."

"That's handy. Who is this guy?"

"His name is Dace."

"Well, that's descriptive. Anything else I should know about him?"

"Oh, he's just a friend, Mom. No one special. In fact, he has a girlfriend, someone I work with."

"Oh, I see. For a moment, I thought... Well, I heard a note in your voice."

"No, no, not me. I'm supposed to swear off men for a while, right?"

"Well, I think you should, honey. Focus on getting your life back. Don't rush into any romances yet."

Kerrie sighed. If only Dace were available, she'd cast her mother's cautionary words to the wind and run into his arms.

"No, Mom. I won't. Not much chance of that here anyway. While I see hundreds of people a day, I don't really meet anyone."

"I know, hon. I talked to the teacher filling in for you at school. The kids really miss you."

Tears welled in Kerrie's eyes. "I miss them too, Mom. I miss my life. Well, no, that's not true. I don't miss most of it. I miss my job and you guys and Suzie."

"We miss you too, honey. I'll say hi to your dad for you. He's in the shower right now."

"Okay, Mom. Thanks for the talk. I'll call again soon."

"Good night, Kerrie."

Kerrie hung up her cell phone and rose to head for the bedroom. She shed her uniform and stepped into a hot steaming shower. There was no time to dwell. She needed to focus on the hike tomorrow and what she would take along. Dace's words of warning were heeded, but she had every intention of continuing her plans.

She slept fitfully that night, her dreams fragmented by bears driving white sports cars around the big top, while ringmaster Dace threw beanbags at Jack attached to a spinning target.

****

Dace lingered in the bookstore after Kerrie left, uncertain of his next move. Had she lied to him? He reviewed his conversation with Sam that afternoon as he'd driven through the gate.

"Hey Dace, wait up." Dace pulled over on the side of the road and waited for Sam to walk up to the vehicle.

"Listen, I was just talking to Mary on the phone and she said I should call you."

Dace grinned. "How is Mary? Are you guys inviting me for dinner or something, a card game, Scrabble?"

Sam rolled his blue eyes. "Funny, Dace. You know what Mary's cooking is like. It almost killed you last time."

"Now, now, Sam, that's just not true. So, what's up?"

"It's Kerrie." Sam appeared agitated.

Dace stiffened.

"What about her?"

"She's going out on a hike again, an overnight to Sperry Chalet, if you can believe it."

"What the—" Dace threw open his car door and jumped out. "Where is she?"

"Now, now, Dace, calm down. She's gone for the day."

"Is she crazy? I don't know what gets into her head sometimes."

Sam shook his head, his arms at his waist. "I don't know either. She sure has a stubborn streak in her."

"Don't I know it," Dace muttered. "Well, did she say what time she was planning on taking off?"

"About seven, I think. Heck, I can't remember if I even got that information out of her. Secretive little gal, that one."

Dace chewed the inside of his mouth. "Yeah, she has good reason to be though."

Sam waited for more information, but nothing

seemed forthcoming.

"Well, you wanted me to let you know if she was going to do anything else foolish, so..." Sam shook his head again and rubbed the back of his neck. "I wasn't sure. I want to protect her rights, but Mary said I'd be a fool not to let you know."

"Thanks, Sam. I'm glad you told me. I'm not sure what I can do about it, but I'm glad you told me." Dace climbed back into his patrol SUV. "I'd better get back on the road. I'll talk to you later."

That was the conversation that prompted Dace to come in search of Kerrie. He could have called her, but somehow...after the last phone call...that seemed like the wrong move.

She'd denied going on a hike in the morning. Maybe, she'd listened to Sam—to the voice of reason—and changed her mind. Dace shook his head. Not likely. She had yet to listen to common sense where her safety was concerned.

He rose from his chair and left the bookstore, wondering how he was going to prevent Kerrie from getting herself into trouble. Had she lied? He hoped not.

****

Kerrie arose bright and early the next morning at 6 a.m. and stowed a change of clothes and food in a backpack. She made sure the bear spray was inside, along with several small flashlights, a rain cover, matches, bug spray, and any other small lightweight things she could think of.

She had made reservations for the chalet that night, a rustic hike-in only hotel built in 1913 by the Great Northern Railway at the end of a seven mile trail. The reservations guaranteed a room and a bed with clean sheets. A hot cooked meal would be available in the dining room. The historic chalet sported no electricity, heat, or running water in the rooms. Only the kitchens and separate restroom buildings provided hot water. She looked forward to her adventure with a mixture of apprehension and excitement.

With a smile and a kiss in Chipper's direction, she drove out to the Park, entering before her coworkers came on duty, and buzzed along Going to the Sun Road past majestic Lake McDonald until she reached the trailhead in the Lake McDonald Lodge parking lot. She strapped on her backpack and headed up the trail, immediately immersing herself in an old growth forest. The trail soon crossed a tiny stream called Midget Creek and began to ascend rather rapidly. Kerrie's calf muscles soon began to burn, forcing her to slow her pace. She stopped occasionally to enjoy the sounds of the forest, the chirping of birds, the gurgling of a nearby stream, and the squeak of an occasional red squirrel as it sensed an intruder.

Kerrie felt at peace with the world and herself as she maneuvered switchbacks on the trail. Sometimes nature had a way of putting things into perspective, of making the chaos of life seem insignificant. She felt like she had truly escaped into the great outdoors, just as brochures on traveling were wont to advertise.

A mile up the trail, she came to a fork and paused to study it carefully. The last thing she wanted was a wrong turn, something she had already done on her last hike, sending her off on another unexpected trail. It had all worked out in the end, but she wanted to waste no energy on any path but the one to the chalet.

The sign pointed the way clearly and she continued her climb, her breath coming in quick gasps, legs continuing to burn. She swatted at the occasional mosquito and considered herself victorious when she actually killed one. A love of all life in general, she had no use for mosquitoes and happily slew all who swarmed near.

Kerrie came around the ridge of the Sprague Creek Valley where the forest changed from cedar and hemlock to pines, firs and larch. Huckleberry bushes abounded and Kerrie pulled off her backpack to rest on a nearby rock. She couldn't resist scouting the bushes for huckleberries, which were laden with the little purple fruit. Hungry and thirsty, she wandered around aimlessly picking huckleberries and popping them in her mouth as she savored the sweet and tart flavor. A nearby rustle in the bushes hardly caught her attention. Another red squirrel disturbed by her presence no doubt.

She heard a low growl, an eerie sound like a moan, and her head shot to the left. There, a hundred yards away, stood a grizzly bear, swaying back and forth as he eyed her. Kerrie's heart stopped and her mouth went dry. She froze in place, desperately trying to remember what she was supposed to do. Freeze? Curl into a fetal position? Run up a tree? Yell? The blonde hair of the bear sparkled in the dappled sunlight as he continued to sway back and forth. He began a panting sound that seemed all the more frightening.

"Back, stay back. Don't come any closer, bear." Kerrie began to back up, keeping her eye on the bear, with no clear idea of where to go. The bear's swaying became more exaggerated, and Kerrie knew the situation was worsening. She couldn't make herself stop backing up. She veiled her eyes so that the bear wouldn't think she was staring him down.

Kerrie longed to scream for help, but felt certain the bear might charge.

"Stay back. I'm leaving. I'm getting out of your berries. See, I'm backing up. Stay back." Kerrie kept mumbling a stream of nonsensical words in monotone as she continued to back up.

She stumbled over the rock holding her backpack, and her eyes flew to the grizzly to gauge his reaction, which was quick in coming. The bear charged suddenly, running through the bushes toward her. Kerrie dropped to a crouch and covered her head with her arms. Through her splayed fingers, she saw the bear veer away at the last moment. He stood to the side, his panting growl deafening and terrifying. Kerrie bit her lip to keep from screaming out. Blood ran into her mouth.

The bear lunged forward again and Kerrie screamed.

At that moment, a shot rang out. Kerrie peeked through the crook of her arm. The bear emitted a high-pitched howl and ran off into the woods as fast as it had come.

Dace dropped to his knees beside Kerrie and huddled beside her while he kept his shotgun pointed in the direction of the fleeing bear. In a flash, the bear was gone. Birds in the surrounding trees chattered nervously for a few moments until the forest fell silent except for the sound of Kerrie's ragged breathing.

"Are you all right?" Dace muttered in a low voice.

"Did you shoot it?" Kerrie lowered her arms and glanced hastily at Dace before turning to scan the forest again. She held her breath the better to hear any rustling bushes.

"With a bean bag, right on its rump."

With the insanity of intense relief, Kerrie leaned into Dace and wrapped her arms around his neck.

"Oh, thank you, thank you. Thank you for not shooting him." Tears fell from her face, tears of relief, fear, reaction, the recession of adrenaline. Her body began to shake as she hid her face in his blue denim shirt.

Dace wrapped his spare around her in a tight grasp. Out of the corner of tear-filled eyes, Kerrie saw he retained his grip on the shotgun.

"Well, you're welcome. I thought you were thanking me for saving you from a savage beast."

Kerrie's watery laugh made her choke on her tears.

"I couldn't stand it if the bear was shot. I just couldn't have." She raised an earnest face to Dace.

He stared down at her with a strange light in his cobalt eyes. In a quick motion, he laid his lips against her forehead. The sweet gesture made her feel safe and secure, as if a beloved parent said good night. She quickly lowered her eyes to the ground, confused, disoriented. Dace cleared his throat.

"It's okay, Kerrie. We don't shoot them just for bluff charges."

"I was eating his huckleberries. I think that's what made him mad," she sniffed and wiped her nose with a shaking hand.

She heard the rumble of Dace's chuckle as she rested on his chest. "Yeah, this is the season and the bears love their huckleberries."

Kerrie studiously admired the front of his shirt and watched the pulse pounding at his throat. A blue shirt... He wasn't in uniform.

She pulled out of his arms, albeit reluctantly, to stare at him.

"What are you doing here? Are you following up on a reported bear sighting? Is that why you're here? You're not in uniform." She noted his dark brown cargo pants and the pack on his back.

"I am as a matter of fact. I'm going to have to call this little fellow in. Someone has to make sure he keeps heading away from the trail." He kept a close watch on the surrounding brush. "Plus...I've been following you."

Kerrie reared back in surprise, lost her balance, and fell over onto her rear end. Dace chuckled and rose to his feet. He offered her his spare hand. She took his hand, but found her legs too wobbly to support her weight. She sat down heavily on the rock that held her backpack.

"What do you mean...you followed me?"

"Hang on. I've got to call this in."

Kerrie watched impatiently as he laid down his backpack and pulled a radio from it, the same radio she'd seen him carry on his hip when in uniform. Why wasn't he in uniform?

"Dispatch, this is thirty-five." He stared into the distance as he waited for a response.

"Go ahead, thirty-five."

"You were right. There is a young grizzly in the area. I'm three miles up on the trail to Sperry Chalet, just west of the ridge to Sprague Creek Valley. We had a bluff charge. I shot him with a bean bag, but you'd better send someone up here to track him in and make sure he stays gone."

"Ten-four, thirty-five, stand by."

Dace lowered his radio and glanced at Kerrie who eyed him suspiciously. The twinkle in his eyes didn't reassure her. What was she supposed to do? Leave and continue her hike? She gulped. Head back down the trail...to defeat. Not likely. Hang out and cling to Dace. A mixed blessing...but to what end?

"Don't even think about it, Kerrie. You're staying right here with me until someone comes to check the area out."

Kerrie said nothing, but hunched her shoulders and crossed her arms. The man was absolutely adorable when he bossed her around like that. She knew he did it for her safety and it bore no resemblance to Jack's controlling behavior. Somehow, she didn't think Sandy suffered orders lightly.

Of course, she had no intention of leaving Dace's side at the moment. The frightening huffing of the grizzly continued to sound in her ears.

A raspy squelching emanating from the radio broke the silence.

"Thirty-five, this is Dispatch."

"Go ahead, Dispatch."

"Bob Hammond is up the trail about three miles heading out from Sperry. He'll take over and secure the trail. ETA is about an hour."

"Affirmative, Dispatch. We'll stand by."

"Dispatch out."

Dace looped his radio on the waistband of his pants and turned to Kerrie.

"Well, we're here to stay for an hour. How about some lunch?"

Kerrie stared at him, waiting for an answer to the mystery.

"You forgot to tell me why you were following me." She tightened her crossed arms and fixed him with a stern look.

"Because I knew you were hiking alone today. You lied to me, Kerrie. I hoped you would tell me the truth last night, but you didn't." He shook his head slightly and braced his shotgun against the rock as he turned to rummage in his bag.

Kerrie felt his disappointment keenly and shame made her hug herself even more tightly. She ducked her head.

"I know I lied. I'm sorry. How did you know I was coming up here?"

"Sam told me. Said he thought it was a bad idea. As it turns out, he was right."

Kerrie's shoulders slumped. She'd struck out alone for a grand adventure, despite warnings from experts, and she'd failed miserably. The vision of a boring and lonely summer loomed before her. If she couldn't hike alone, what was she going to do? Her work schedule simply did not permit her to join any weekend hiking groups.

"Hey, how come you're not working today? Do you always carry a shotgun with you when you hike?"

Dace grinned as he pulled a sandwich out of his bag. He sat down on the rock and offered her half of his food. Kerrie shook her head and rummaged in her own bag for her sandwich.

"I'm not working today. This is my weekend. Didn't you know that? You and I share the same days off. They switched my schedule a while ago. And no, I don't carry a shotgun on hikes. I checked in at headquarters before I came up here. They reported a grizzly sighting on the trail yesterday evening and asked if I'd take the gun up and check out the area while I made my way up to the chalet."

"Who is this Bob Hammond?"

"He's a back country ranger. Stays out here for about ten days at a time, then goes back in for four. He probably knows this young grizzly well."

"I can't imagine living out here for ten days at a time." She shivered and surveyed the thick brush.

"It's rough, but some of them love it. I did it for my first two years with the Park, but I prefer daily showers, so I moved back down to the flatlands."

Kerrie munched on her sandwich with a sideways look at Dace. "I didn't know we had the same days off. I should have realized since I see you come through the gate every day I'm there."

He tilted his head and grinned. "*I* knew it."

Kerrie blushed and ignored him. She just didn't understand him sometimes. Was he flirting or simply that charming?

"So, what's the plan? I'd still like to get up to Sperry Chalet. I have reservations tonight. When the back country ranger comes, will it be safe for me to make my way up?"

Dace nodded, popping the last of his food into his mouth. "Sure. I'll be with you. I'm going to leave the shotgun for Bob though."

Kerrie bit her lip. "Dace, you don't have to go with me. It's a long hike. What? Are you going to turn around and head back down tonight?"

Dace gazed at her for a moment, his lips twitching. "No, I don't think so. I'll stay the night at the chalet. If it's full, I'll stay in the campground. Got my pup tent here." He carelessly gestured toward his well-used backpack, which seemed much larger and more tightly packed than hers.

Kerrie clamped her mouth shut on further

protestations. She knew Dace well enough by now to realize he wouldn't change his mind. She also realized that she was fairly well on her way to falling in love with him. He epitomized everything she wanted in a man—strength without cruelty, easy laughter without mocking, kindness without manipulation. That he was heartbreakingly handsome did not hurt.

She stared at him as he dragged a bottle of water from his bag, but dropped her eyes when he turned toward her.

"How are you feeling now? Better? Getting over the shakes?"

"Yes, I am. I think I heard a story about you once...that you'd been attacked by a grizzly sow."

Dace gave a snort of mirthless humor. "Yeah. That one didn't bother with a bluff charge. She just barreled right into me. That happened during that first year as a back country ranger. Man, the mosquitoes were heavy that year." He slapped the back of his neck at an imaginary blood-sucking pest.

"And?" Kerry prompted.

"And I was hiking down a trail when she flew out of the bushes right at me. Out of the corner of my eye, I barely saw her two cubs dash behind a tree. She launched herself at me and pinned me down. I had my hands full trying to protect my face and couldn't get to the pepper spray strapped to my hip. She took a good hunk of my arm and shook it for a few seconds, but I managed to get a burst of spray off in her face, and she took off. The cubs ran after her."

"Wow," Kerry breathed inarticulately. "How is your arm?"

"Fine now. Took thirty stitches to close, but..."

She gazed at his exposed lower arms, but saw no scars.

"Was it on your upper arm?"

"Yeah. Here."

He removed his outer shirt to reveal a fairly tight green T-shirt. Kerry ogled his well defined muscular chest. He indicated a large crescent shaped scar on his left upper arm that ran approximately ten inches.

Dace glanced down at it ruefully as he pulled his

shirt back on. "Luckily, she didn't get any tendons. So, it's all better now." He flashed her a bright grin.

"Did they go after her? You know, hunt her down. I heard when bears actually attack humans, they—"

"No, not this one. She was just a grizzly sow protecting her cubs and she was in the back country...not near a campground or anything. It was her territory and she did what came naturally. She could have killed me in the time it took to get my pepper spray out, but she didn't."

Kerrie longed to lay her lips against his arm, to lay her head against his chest and listen to his heartbeat as she had earlier. She swallowed hard. Sandy! Sandy would most certainly object. Kerrie had never stolen a man away from a woman yet, wouldn't know how to go about it, and didn't have the gumption for such underhanded behavior. She sighed heavily. Sandy was such a lucky woman.

"Now, don't go sighing over the bear. She got her way. I got the heck off her trail pronto."

A gurgle of laughter erupted from Kerrie's throat as she met Dace's laughing eyes. He burst out in laughter. Kerrie grabbed his arm in a cautionary warning.

"Shhhh," she continued to giggle. "*This* bear might come back."

Dace chuckled. "The more noise we make, the better it is. Bears don't like to be surprised. You probably surprised this fella. He'll stay away as long as he hears us talking."

"What's all that racket, Mitchell?"

Just then, a stocky, well built man in a Park Service utility uniform came around the corner of the path. His weather-beaten skin reflected hours spent under the sun. Brown eyes glinted as he raised a hand to his thick handlebar mustache and grinned. He was accompanied by a younger, slim man in a ranger uniform sporting a beginner beard.

"So, you had another run in, is that right, Dace?"

"Hey, Bob. Glad to see you. You sure made it here fast." Dace stood up and put an arm around the older man's shoulders. "Kerrie, this is my first boss here at Glacier, Bob Hammond." Dace grinned affectionately at the older sturdy man. "He taught me everything I know about the back country."

"Which isn't much apparently, you idiot. What's this I hear about a bluff charge?"

"Yeah, some young grizzly objected to Kerrie's presence and ran at her. I was just down the trail and heard the commotion, arrived in time to see him charge her and veer away. It seemed clear he wasn't planning on having her for lunch. I had the bean bag shotgun with me and sent one to his rump on his second charge. He took off into the bushes about forty-five minutes ago. You made good time getting here." He patted Bob on the back.

"Well, good thing I did, too. I'm pretty sure you've bungled the whole thing. At least you didn't get yourself half-eaten this time. Luckily, this young cub, Daniel here, has me to protect him."

Kerrie, who had risen with Dace, began to object, but Dace grinned and laughed. Daniel's face reddened as he grinned accommodatingly.

"Yeah, no doubt you would have done a better job wrestling him to the ground, old bear ranger that you are."

"Darn tootin'." Bob grinned at Kerrie, seemingly aware she had taken offense to his teasing. "Well, who is this anyway? You might want to stick with me, gal. This man's only gonna get you in trouble."

Convinced by the twinkle in his eye that he held Dace in the deepest affection, she relaxed to his gruff demeanor and grinned.

"Now, now, Bob. Don't make me tell Kathy. I saw her down at the campground the other day. She said she's ready to leave you and take off with me because at least I come home at night."

Bob grinned, his teeth white under his thick mustache.

"She's been saying that for...what...ten years now? She still ain't gone. Keeps coming back here every season with me. Loves that campground of hers. Keeps those campers ship shape and on the straight and narrow."

"She does that, all right." Dace laughed once again with a slight wink in Kerrie's direction. Her knees weakened at the gesture.

"Well, Bob, we'd better get up the trail if we're going

to get there anytime before dark. Here's the gun. It's all yours. You get to haul it around for a while now."

"Gee, thanks, Dace. It's not like I really need it anyway. You know all I have to do is tell the bear to "sit" and he will. I'm that good." Bob grabbed the gun and passed it to the silent, but attentive, Daniel as he headed into the brush. Bob stopped to study the ground for a moment before moving off.

"See ya soon. I'll clean up your mess here." He yelled over his shoulder. His younger companion gave them a parting wave and followed the older man into the trees.

"Thanks, boss," Dace yelled with a chuckle as he hoisted his pack onto his back. He glanced down at a pensive Kerrie. "Are you ready?"

Kerrie nodded and heaved her pack onto her back. Dace leaned over to help her slip it onto her shoulder. His hand lingered there a moment before he dropped it and Kerrie longed to rub her face against his hand like a kitten.

Dace cleared his throat and led the way up the path. Kerrie followed, once again admiring his relaxed gait and the strength of his legs as he easily ascended the trail. Fortunately, the path leveled out for the next several miles. Dace turned occasionally to see how Kerrie was doing. She felt at once cared for and babied, enjoying the one and resenting the other. She swatted at an occasional mosquito and began to work up a head of steam as resentment began to win the day. She was sick and tired of staring at the backside of the man she had fallen in love with. She couldn't have him so what was the point. He turned once again to check on her, a nurturing and kind expression on his face. That was it!

"You know, Dace. I'm okay back here. Remember, I was making this hike on my own."

He kept up the pace, but spoke over his shoulder. "That didn't really work out too well, Kerrie."

Kerrie gritted her teeth. He was right, of course, but...

"Thanks for pointing that out. It was a fluke. I've hiked by myself before without any trouble."

Dace stopped in the middle of the path and turned. Kerrie, her head down to watch her footing, bumped into him. He reached out to steady her. She jumped back as she always seemed to do these days, and he dropped his hands.

"Sorry." He muttered with a rueful shake of his head. "You sound mad. What's up?"

"Nothing." Kerrie stared at the ground, chewing the inside of her lip. "I just don't want to be babied, that's all."

"Man, *I* do." Teasing laughter lit up his voice. "I'd love to be babied." He let go an exaggerated sigh.

"This isn't funny. I feel silly having you hike all the way up to Sperry. I should have turned around back there and headed down. I can always do this another day."

Dace's brow furrowed as he studied her face. "Well, actually, it's pretty hard to get reservations at the chalet. You won't get another chance to stay there if you haven't made those plans already. That's why I might have to stay in the campground." He reached out a tentative hand. "What's wrong, Kerrie?"

She stopped just short of stomping her foot...just short. "Nothing. I'm hot and I'm tired and the mosquitoes are biting me and all I can see of the trail is your backside."

Taken aback for a moment, Dace burst into laughter. He slipped his backpack off his heaving shoulders and rested it against a tree, kneeling down to open the pack and retrieve some water and a bottle of mosquito repellant.

"And I thought my backside was one of my best features," he murmured mournfully as he moved toward Kerrie.

Chapter Ten

"Very funny," Kerrie fumed. She stared at Dace with a flaming face and suspicious eyes as he gently removed her pack from her back. He handed her the bottle of water and poured insect repellent into his open palm. The feel of his hand on the back and sides of her neck as he smoothed the lemon-scented liquid onto her skin sent shivers up her spine and weakened her already shaky legs. She faltered momentarily.

"Here, sit down. You look exhausted. Drink some water." Dace lowered her to sit on his pack under the tree. He dropped down beside her on one knee and took one of her hands to smooth repellent over the exposed skin. Kerrie watched his bent dark head tenderly. She had to get away from this man. He raised sensuous eyes to study her face as he finished rubbing the liquid on the back of her other hand.

"How's that?" He grinned quickly and sat down beside her on the ground. "I know you told me not to baby you, but..." He paused and swallowed some water from the bottle she handed back to him. "It's hard to resist. You look like you need taking care of."

Kerrie stiffened. Humiliation washed over her. She felt like such a failure. She sighed.

"Dace, while I may look like I need to be coddled, I don't. I'm a lot tougher than I look...at least I hope I am."

He turned gentle eyes on her. "I know you're strong, Kerrie. Women who've lived through abuse have to be tough. Otherwise, they wouldn't survive." He turned away and stared out over the valley for a moment. "Maybe it's just me. Maybe *I'm* the one who needs someone to baby."

Kerrie turned startled eyes on him. His bronze cheeks took on a reddish hue. He gave her a quick wink and took a swallow of water. A mischievous imp possessed Kerrie.

"Maybe you should have children," she quipped.

He looked at her quickly, a daring glint in his eyes. "Are you volunteering to help?"

Hoist with her own petard as they say, Kerrie sputtered, "Oh, for Pete's sake, Dace. I can't believe you said that."

His full-bodied laugh resounded across the valley. "I know. Crass, wasn't it?" He shook his head without the slightest hint of repentance. "I would have had children if I could have found a woman who wanted to roam around with me enough to get married. I can't stay still. I think I told you that." He paused for a swallow of water. "How about you, Kerrie? Do you like to travel?" He fixed her with an intent gaze, cobalt eyes sparkling like diamonds on dark blue velvet.

Kerrie eyed him suspiciously for a moment. Something in those diamonds seemed to reach out to her, but she couldn't...or wouldn't read anything into his expression. She reassured herself that he simply made prosaic conversation.

She shook her head. "I don't know. This is the furthest I've been from home. I'm a mama's girl, I guess. I miss my family. I feel homesick sometimes."

Dace stared hard at her for a moment, then turned to gaze out over the valley. She hoped she hadn't sounded too whiney. Her departure had been so abrupt that she didn't feel she was exploring a new place so much as escaping the past. Maybe she *did* like to travel. How did she know?

"It sounds like you like enjoy staying in one place." Dace rose, his voice husky. "Good for you. I don't know what it's like to be firmly settled." He held out a hand to help her rise.

They resumed their hike, climbing once again up a series of switchbacks through a serene, cool alpine forest within constant view of a spectacular waterfall that cascaded down the rocky mountainside. Kerrie would have loved to stand at the foot of the falls and allow the spray to cool her down, but they were near the top of the foamy white waterfall, and the idea of climbing back up again did not appeal.

They passed out of sight and sound of the tantalizing waterfall and continued ever on and upward. When the forest thinned out, Dace paused on the path.

"Look," he pointed. Kerrie followed his direction and saw several green-roofed chalets perched high on a cliff to the right.

"Are we there yet?" She tried to keep the panting out of her speech.

He turned and grinned sympathetically. "Not yet, we've still got quite a climb. Breathe in! Can't you smell the fresh mountain air? Isn't it great?"

It was all Kerrie could do to gasp, but she did as he requested and dragged in a breath through her nose. The alpine air did smell pure and clean, unlike any "fresh air" she'd ever known.

"You're short of breath because of the altitude. We're at about 6,500 feet. Just take your time."

He moved out slowly, but stopped abruptly. "Shhhh."

"What?" she whispered, fear seizing her heart and stealing her last breath. She moved toward Dace and butted up to him for safety.

"Not a bear. Look, a mountain goat." He pointed to the path up ahead where two white creatures wandered. "It's a nanny and her kid."

"Ohhhh, how cute," Kerrie whimpered helplessly. The nanny, a fuzzy white creature with tiny horns sprouting from her head, stopped for a moment and turned to stare at the intruders on the path. The baby goat nestled against her, peeking around with large dark eyes to survey the scene.

The nanny cast a last assessing glance at them before she turned off the path and began to ascend the cliff. Kerrie stared in awe as the mountain goat and her adorable youngster nonchalantly clambered straight up the side of the impossibly steep embankment.

"How do they do that?" Kerrie caught her breath.

"I have no idea," Dace murmured. "They eat the moss and lichen on the rocks of the steep inclines."

"This is so beautiful." Kerrie sighed in contentment as she expanded her lungs to draw in more of the thin air.

"We'd better head up. The last part of the climb is the steepest."

"That's just not possible," Kerry muttered, though the sight of the mountain goats had invigorated her.

They crossed a footbridge over Sperry Creek and staggered up to the nearest building, the dining room where Kerrie was to check in. With burning legs and lungs, Kerrie wrestled herself out of her pack and collapsed onto a wooden bench outside the entrance, gazing out over the valley below. From this height, she could see views of turquoise Lake McDonald, some 7 miles ago and 3,300 feet below.

Dace dropped his bag and sat beside her.

"I'm going to wait to see you checked in. The hotel is up the hill there, so you still have a bit more to go." He reached over and casually brushed a limp curl which dangled unheeded in front of her nose. Too exhausted to relish the moment, Kerrie stored the memory away for future dwelling. "When you're settled, I'll head out to the campground unless they've got room for me here."

"Well, I hope they do. Unless you *want* to camp."

"I don't mind setting up the tent, but frankly, my bones are creaking a bit right now too. I wouldn't mind sinking into a nice soft mattress."

An uncomfortable twinge of guilt forced Kerrie to her feet.

"Well, let me go see."

Dace left his pack outside and followed her in. As he had predicted, they had no extra rooms for him.

"I'm sorry, Dace." She stared up at him in consternation.

"That's okay, Kerrie. I'll be fine."

"Where is the campground?" she fretted although she didn't know why. "How far is it?"

He pointed further up the hill. "It's just up there, past the hotel, about a fifteen minute walk."

"I don't see it," she said fretfully, scanning the hillside above.

He turned and faced her. "You sound worried, Kerrie. Are you afraid to stay up here by yourself? It's perfectly safe. I'll hike back out with you tomorrow. In fact, we can have dinner together tonight in the dining room if that's all right with you."

Kerrie stiffened. "I'm not worried about *me*. I just feel bad there's no room for you at the chalet, after you came all the way up here with me."

Dace grinned. “Well, thanks for the concern, but I’ll be fine. Shall we head up to your room? Check it out?”

“Oh, I can manage, Dace, really.”

“Come on, let me walk up with you. It’s on the way. They’ve done some renovations on the place and I’d like to see them.”

“Okay,” she murmured, as she attempted to subdue the thrill that he would continue to remain in her presence for a while longer.

They made their way up the hill, past the new restroom building and a maintenance building, and approached the Swiss-style chalet built of native rock and trimmed with rough hewn logs. Mountain peaks towered around the chalet on all sides. Kerrie found her assigned quarters and entered the cozy room graced with varnished wooden floors and rustic rock walls. There was no electricity or heat and no bathroom, but the simple queen-sized bed with its red-striped bedspread appeared comfortable. The late afternoon sun streamed in through the curtained windows, taking the chill off the room.

“It’ll probably get cold in here tonight. Did you bring something warm to sleep in?”

Kerrie nodded. “Oh yes, and two flashlights. I read in the brochure that we can’t have candles.”

“No, I guess not.” Dace surveyed the room. “Well, everything looks pretty nice. I’m going to head out and up to the campground in case it fills up and I don’t get a spot. I didn’t reserve one, so I’ll have to sweet talk Bob when he heads back up to let me grab a spot.”

“That doesn’t sound promising.”

“I’ll be fine. I’ll see you around 6 p.m. at the dining room, okay?”

“Okay, see you then.”

Dace walked out the door, and Kerrie crossed over to the window to stare down the valley below. She had a magnificent view from her window, but it seemed somehow less spectacular in Dace’s absence. She checked her watch. Only an hour until dinner. Kerrie decided on a change of clothes and rummaged through her bag for a fresh pair of trousers, a T-shirt, and a sweatshirt. She pulled out her jacket and donned it as well. The temperature dropped rapidly in the short time she had been there, and her fertile imagination supplied an image of Dace in his pup tent in the middle of the night, shivering, his teeth chattering as his body craved warmth.

Kerrie shook her head with a sheepish grin. Ridiculous! Dace was a big boy, and he was hardly her big boy to worry about. She wondered what Sandy would think of this little adventure.

She wandered outside to survey the scenery. A wooden deck which ran along the length of the hotel provided a wonderful place to sit and admire the view of the alpine forest and surrounding meadow. A few other guests took photographs and admired the vista, and she contentedly listened to the hum of their conversation as she searched the tree line for mountain goats.

Occasional snatches of sentences made their way to her ears though she tried not to eavesdrop. A middle-aged man in a blue sweater and jeans and his companion, a similarly-aged woman in a fleece jacket and slacks, leaned against the railing nearby. The word *bear* caught her attention as it probably would for the rest of her life. She shamelessly turned an ear toward the man to hear his words.

"You know, those girls who were mauled by grizzlies. One of the attacks was in the campground near the chalet...right below the chalet."

Kerrie stiffened. Grizzlies? Up here? Dace was staying in the campground. Had there been an attack? She held her breath and strained to hear, though the pounding in her heart blocked some words.

"Yeah, it was horrible. That same night, another grizzly attacked and killed another girl in a campground ten miles away. They said it couldn't be the same grizzly." Impatiently, she brushed her hair away from her ears. "Snatched her right out of her sleeping bag in the campground."

Kerrie turned to stare at the couple. Their faces showed no fear, though the woman's eyes were round. The man shook his head slightly and they turned to move off.

Kerrie's first instinct was to rush after them, demanding to know the full story, but her legs seemed numb. She couldn't move. Weakness pervaded her very being, and she stared at their retreating backs helplessly.

An image of Dace being dragged off by a grizzly bear tore at her heart. She gritted her teeth. Dace couldn't sleep in the campground tonight! Maybe he hadn't heard about the attacks. He would have to sleep in her room. She would insist.

The irritating voice of conscience sat on her shoulder and pondered.

Kerrie, are you sure you just don't want to get him into your room? Does this have anything to do with bears?

She ignored the obnoxious voice. Bears were a real and present danger. She knew. After all, a bear had charged her that very morning. Maybe it wasn't always a bluff!

Kerrie finally found the gumption to push herself off the bench and anxiously head toward the dining room. Her legs ached from the hike and an occasional tremor ran through her knees. She stumbled a few times on her way down the hill but managed to stay on her feet.

She arrived at the dining room shortly before six. Several other guests, including the couple she overheard discussing the bear attacks, milled about the closed entrance to the dining room. Dace was not among them.

Kerrie paced restlessly along the outside of the rustic gray stone building, her attention momentarily diverted by the sight of several mountain goats lounging in the late afternoon sun on nearby rock outcroppings. She paused to watch them. They certainly weren't skittish around humans.

"I wondered if they still hung out here. It's been several years since I've been all the way up to the chalet."

Kerrie jumped at the sound of Dace's voice behind her. She swung around and grabbed the front of his jacket.

"Dace, Dace." She swallowed hard, trying to catch her breath, cut short by anxiety.

Dace's bright blue-gray eyes widened and he covered her hands with his own.

"Did you miss me, Kerrie?" A small smile spread across his face.

"Bear attacks. Did you hear about them?"

His smile vanished and he stared hard at her. His grip on her hands tightened.

"What are you talking about? When? I would have heard something on my radio." The silent radio hung from his belt loop.

"No, not today...at least I don't think so. I don't know when." Kerrie's fingers relaxed in his secure grip and she unconsciously laid her hands flat across his chest. "I overhead some people talking about grizzly attacks, one in the campground. You can't stay there. You have to stay down here with me...in a secure building. There's only one bed, but we'll figure it out." Kerrie babbled nervously, exquisitely aware of the seductive feel of Dace's warm hands on hers.

To her astonishment, Dace pulled her into his arms and pressed her head against his shoulder. He held her tightly as he whispered against her hair.

"Kerrie, Kerrie, you poor thing. I think I know what you're talking about. Those attacks were over forty years ago." Dace lifted his head and stared down into Kerrie's startled face. He loosened his grip on her but did not let go.

"One was far from here at a place called Trout Lake. They closed that campground and never reopened it. The other one was over at Granite Park campground. Back in the day, they used to bait the bears down by the garbage dumpsters...so the tourists could see the grizzlies coming to eat. There'd never been any fatal maulings before then. But in August 1967, one grizzly did attack a young couple in the campground and hauled the woman off. The rangers tracked down both bears eventually and killed them, and they stopped the policy of leaving food out so folks could see the bears." He sighed heavily. "We've gotten smarter since then in our bear management practices...at least I hope we have. There's nothing to worry about now."

Kerrie quirked a skeptical eyebrow before she resumed watching his lips move. He'd kissed her with those lips...well, on the head, of course, but still...

He grinned sheepishly. "Okay, I mean there's always something to worry about. I'm not saying grizzlies haven't been known to attack since then."

Kerrie's bemused eyes moved from his lips back to his eyes. She raised her eyebrow once again at his words.

"Okay, you've got me there. It's never completely safe, but there have been no fatalities from grizzly bear maulings at Glacier for years."

"How many years?"

Dace furrowed his brow. "I don't know. Ten years?"

"I thought you said the attacks were in 1967. So, there have been more?"

Dace winced. "A few...here in the Park. And Yellowstone. Canada usually has more."

"Hmmppff." Kerrie pulled out of his arms, albeit reluctantly. "It's a horrible story and I still don't think it's safe. You're welcome to share my room. You can spread your sleeping bag out on the floor or we can take turns sleeping on the bed." Her cheeks flushed, and she reminded herself that she was concerned about his safety. She felt certain she wouldn't sleep a wink that night—whether he slept in the campground...or in the room.

Dace leaned back against the wooden log railing and crossed his arms. He tilted his head and studied her face. She stared over his shoulder at a spot in the distance...anything other than meet his eyes.

"Okay, we'll give it a try. But I'm pretty sure you'll throw me out once you hear me snore."

Kerrie peeked over at him. "Do you snore?"

Dace shrugged, a teasing grin lighting his face. "I don't know. You'll have to tell me."

Kerrie gave a slight shake of her head, a small smile breaking through. Her eyes traveled past him up to the direction of the campground, her thoughts dwelling on the horror at the Granite Chalet campground so many years ago. Her face drooped as she shuddered and hugged herself tightly. She could have suffered the same fate as that poor girl...only hours ago.

Dace moved toward her quickly and put a safe arm around her shoulders. "Come on, let's go in for dinner." As if on cue, a loud bell pealed out announcing dinner, its echo reverberating over the surrounding mountains.

Dace walked Kerrie inside the dining room. Six tables of varying sizes covered with plastic covered pink table cloths gave the room an outdoorsy picnic feel. They found their assigned seating at one of the smaller tables set for four near a window framed by rose-patterned curtains.

Kerrie settled in her lightweight wicker style chair with wonder.

“Dace, how do they get all this stuff up here? Helicopter? Is there a service road of some sort?”

Dace chuckled. “Not likely. No, they pack it in with mules. Every single piece. That’s how the railroad managed to build the place in 1913.”

Kerrie surveyed the room in awe. Large gleaming trusses supported the shingled roof and lorded it over the exposed stone walls. Varnished wooden floors gleamed under the bright lights. A massive fireplace dominated the east wall and hosted a toasty fire which removed the chill from the building with no central heating.

“It’s a great building, isn’t it?”

“It is,” Kerrie breathed. “I’m so glad I managed to get up here.” She cast him a look from under veiled lashes. “With your help, of course.”

“Ah, think nothing of it. I enjoyed the hike. It’s been a while.”

Kerrie decided on a frontal attack.

“Doesn’t Sandy hike?”

“Sandy?” He furrowed his brow and glanced around the room at the arriving guests. “Yeah, she hikes occasionally. I don’t think she really likes it though. Kayaking is her thing.”

“Oh,” Kerrie murmured ineffectively, remembering Sandy had told her the same thing. “Do you kayak?”

“Yeah, occasionally. Though it’s been a while since I did that as well.” He eyed her with a grin on his face. “Now, I’m not one of these whitewater sorts. I prefer the placid serenity of Lake McDonald. Call me old and set in my ways.”

The waiter arrived with their first course, pasta salad and pumpkin bread, both of which looked delicious.

“Do you like to kayak, Kerrie?”

Through a bite of pumpkin bread, Kerrie mumbled. “I don’t know. I’ve never tried it.”

“Maybe Sandy can take you out some time...or you can come with me on the tame plan.” Dace looked down at his salad and moved it around the plate.

Kerrie swallowed hard, and with the bread stuck in

her throat, it hurt.

"Oh." She took a deep breath. "Sandy did invite me...in a casual way...a long time ago. The subject hasn't come up since."

"I see." He looked at her sharply and then down at a piece of bread in his hand. "Well, like I said, if you like it slow..."

Kerrie watched as Dace's face reddened. His comment *did* seem rather suggestive. Her own face flamed, but she couldn't resist the obvious comeback.

"I do like it slow, Dace." Having spit her comment out and aghast at her brazenness, she reached for her water to gulp down half the glass, hoping she wouldn't choke as a round of nervous giggles erupted.

Dace's eyes widened and he threw her a startled look before he burst into deep laughter, one hand clutching his ribs. Neighboring heads turned toward them, smiling at the merriment.

Dace caught his breath. "I think I'm going to have to watch my step with you, Kerrie. You have hidden depths I never suspected."

Kerrie slapped a hand over her mouth to stifle her laughter...and any more outrageous comments.

"Oh, just ignore me, Dace. I'm sure I'm just tired from the hike and the stress of the bear charge."

His laughter died down, but a glint in his eye and a slow smile on his lips should have warned Kerrie.

"I can't ignore you. I've tried. It didn't work out."

"What?"

They were interrupted by the arrival of a hot tomato basil soup and removal of the salad dishes. Kerrie returned her gaze to Dace, who lowered his eyes and made a production of stirring his soup with a spoon. Ignore her? Would he explain?

He glanced up at her with a sheepish grin. "You know. When I didn't talk to you for those few weeks...after I grabbed you in the parking lot...for which I'm still ashamed by the way. We never did get our dinner that night."

Kerrie blinked and stared down into her soup. What could she say? Unable to make any sense of the conversation, she opted to ignore it. It became more and more obvious that Dace was not as firmly committed to Sandy as he should be. And though Kerrie was head over heels in love with him, she had no use for a man who cheated. If he did it once, he would do it again. She took a deep breath. Too bad she hadn't learned that lesson sooner with Jack and his fists.

"Kerrie?"

"Hmmm?" Kerrie slurped her soup with gusto, hoping to appear busy.

"Did you hear me?"

She sighed and put her spoon down. She glanced at him through lowered lashes, desperately trying to avoid reading anything into his eyes.

"Yes, Dace. I heard your words. I don't understand them very well...or maybe I don't want to...so I'm ignoring them." She gave him a bright smile and returned her attention to her food. He would remain on the pedestal she had built for him come rain or shine.

"Oh," he copied her favorite silence filler. Out of the corner of her eye, she watched him lay his soup spoon down and sit back in his chair. She stole a peek at his face. He stared out the window, a frown on his face.

The waiter brought the rest of their meal, a summer Thanksgiving treat of turkey, dressing and mashed potatoes. The food looked delicious, but something had gone out of the meal.

"So, I have no chance with you." The flat statement seemed to be a question.

Kerrie stopped ogling her meal and turned troubled eyes on Dace's grave face.

"No."

Chapter Eleven

"No." Kerrie mustered up all her strength and shook her head firmly. She looked away and bit her lip to stop it from trembling. He would remain her hero, and she would help him do it. Her hero was faithful to his woman—loyal, kind, strong, and humorous. Dace possessed all of those qualities, though he seemed to be struggling with the first.

Her voice was hushed when she spoke. "I think I've been leaning on you too much. You know, with Jack and the abuse and the bear and all." She couldn't meet his eyes and spoke to her plate. "I think you believe I need a knight in shining armor, and you've come to my rescue."

"That's not—"

"Wait, let me finish. You're chivalrous, and you're a protector. And a wonderful one at that." She sighed on her last words. "But I'm tough. You said so yourself. I'm going to be fine. I don't need a hero." She kept her eyes veiled by her lashes. She lied. Of course, she needed a hero, and Dace was it. After Jack, any man would be heroic. She loved Dace for every wonderful quality he possessed, but she had no intention of allowing him to cheat on Sandy because he felt compelled to take care of a strange lonely woman.

"Just a min—" Dace raised a hand in protest.

"Remember? You said maybe you need to baby someone, but I'm not that someone, Dace."

"I see," Dace murmured, his voice flat, emotionless. Kerrie cringed as he quietly pushed back his chair, laid enough money to cover both meals on the table and walked out of the dining room. She felt like she had ruined their lovely meal, although realistically, perhaps it was he who had spoiled the evening with his direct question. No. She was at fault. Perhaps they both were.

Kerrie shook her head and rose from her seat slowly, her appetite lost. She made her way outside the dining room, hoping Dace lingered on the balcony. Only the mountain goats remained outside. Unsure what to do with herself, she turned to head back up the hill to the dormitory part of the hotel.

Kerrie entered her room and moved over to the window. The sun had disappeared over the expanse of Lake McDonald 3,300 feet below and dusk cast shadows along the tree line. It seemed likely that Dace no longer considered himself welcome in her room. Kerrie snorted aloud. How untrue that was! She couldn't rid herself of the worry that he wasn't safe up there. The knowledge that the campground had been popular for years made no dent in her fears. She leaned on the railing and stared over the valley. The memory of the bear charging her that morning would not soon disappear, and the images elicited by the story of the grizzly attacks forty years ago made her queasy. What if something happened to Dace?

She argued with herself. Dace was a trained bear ranger. He knew how to handle himself. He certainly knew the proper techniques for storing food and camping in the wilderness. Still, she was in love and that made him vulnerable. He was something...or someone to be cherished. If nothing else, she couldn't bear the thought of him sleeping in the cold when she had a comfortable, albeit unheated, room to share.

Kerrie fought with herself and lost. She headed out of the dormitory to find the campground. Large shadows grew as she headed for the back of the dormitory, and she cursed herself for giving in to her desires.

Darkness rapidly descended, but Kerrie could hear voices coming from the campground and she pointed herself in that general direction, the glow of the quarter moon giving little help. Away from the lights of the chalet, her plan to find Dace seemed glaringly stupid and she hesitated as she stumbled over a boulder. Tall pine trees rustled in the stiff cold wind which seemed to suddenly spring up.

Kerrie heard a sound nearby and froze. Without conscious thought, she crouched down to her knees and held her breath. A bear! A dark shape materialized out of the darkness and headed for her. Kerrie covered her head with her hands and screamed. The animal brushed her, cursed, and stopped in its tracks.

"Good gravy, Kerrie. What are you doing out here?"

Dace reached for her in the darkness, connecting with the hands covering her head.

"Woman, don't tell me you don't need a babysitter. You make some of the worst decisions concerning your safety. What are you doing out here? Kerrie?"

Kerrie weakly sank to the ground, and Dace knelt down beside her as well as he could in the darkness. He pulled her hands from her head and held them in a firm grip. A muffle sob escaped her lips and she clamped her mouth shut on it, though she desperately needed to breathe.

"Kerrie? Are you all right?"

"Yes," she gasped. Another rustle in a nearby pine tree made her whimper.

"Did you think I was another bear?"

She nodded, uncaring that he couldn't see her face.

"I'll take that as a yes." Dace sighed heavily. "Well, you should, woman. Haven't you had enough excitement for one day?"

"I was coming to find you."

"Why? Did you lose me?"

Kerrie refused to chuckle. It was close to the truth.

"No, I just felt so bad. I worried about you up there in the campground." Her teeth chattered from fear and the cold night wind.

To her dismay and utter delight, Dace reached over and pulled her to him as he lowered himself to the ground. Something soft fell beside them.

"Well, as it happens, I was headed down to the hotel with my sleeping bag anyway. I told you I'd stay there and I'm not one to break my word." His voice was gruff as he spoke over the top of her head. "I imagine you'll probably have nightmares tonight anyway and I wanted to be there to help."

Kerrie pressed into him, the racing in her heart taking on a different rhythm. She was in his arms, and the thrill of it did nothing to help her body calm down.

She mumbled into his coat. "You're probably right. Maybe I do need a babysitter...for a wile." She tried to see his face in the dark. "Just for a while."

"Just for a while," he murmured against her hair. "Where's your flashlight? I didn't even see a light on the path."

Kerrie gulped. "I...uh...didn't bring one. It was still light when I left the room."

"Hmmm..." Dace had the grace not to rub in her foolish behavior any further. "Well, come on, let's get you back. It's getting cold out here in the wind." He pulled Kerrie up and held onto her hand as he picked up his sleeping bag.

He turned on his flashlight and led her carefully down the trail toward the chalet.

"Why didn't I see your flashlight on the trail? The light might have warned me it wasn't a bear," she asked in a suspicious tone.

"I...uh...I didn't have it on. Thought I knew where I was going."

"Hah!" she muttered.

"Touché," he murmured.

They reached the outskirts of the hotel grounds. Small lights glimmered in several of the rooms. It seemed other residents read or played cards by the light of their flashlights. Dace led the way to her room and Kerrie opened the door. The room had grown cold, and Kerrie longed to jump into her pajamas and huddle under the covers for warmth. She found her flashlight and turned it on, with an uncertain glance in Dace's direction.

"Go ahead," he said. "I'll turn my back and spread out my sleeping bag over in this corner."

"Do you want to swap out and take the bed in a few hours? I can share. It's only fair."

Dace chuckled, busily setting up his overnight accommodations. "No, I'll be fine. I wouldn't dream of putting you on the floor. I'm the tough bear ranger, remember?"

Kerrie quickly changed clothing and jumped into the large bed. It seemed such a pity that they couldn't share the bed, but... Still, she mused, it seemed a waste of good, soft mattress.

She watched Dace settle onto the floor and turn off his flashlight.

"Good night, Kerrie. Sleep well."

“Good night, Dace. I hope it’s not too hard down there.”

“No harder than it has to be, Kerrie.” She could barely hear his husky voice.

Kerrie burrowed down into the covers and closed her eyes...for about five seconds. Fairly sure she wasn’t going to be able to sleep a wink that night, she turned on her side and stared out the window. Moonlight shone in the room, casting an eerie glow on the varnished wooden floors. She could see Dace’s form in the corner, and she listened for the sound of his breathing. Would she know when he fell into a deep sleep? Did he snore? Her lips curved in a tender smile. He was such a charming enigma. She didn’t understand him in the least.

She stood by the side of a beautiful pristine lake, its glacial waters a milky turquoise hue. Mountains surrounded the lake on all sides, as if it were the crater of a volcano which erupted long ago. Hawks soared overhead and a lone buck stood by the bank on the other side of the lake calmly lowering his majestic antlered head to drink. A huffing sound behind her broke the silence and she swung around to see a blonde grizzly bear charging her. She froze in place. The bear was just bluffing. He would veer away at the last moment. But the bear didn’t veer away, and Kerrie screamed as he launched himself at her, his growl deafening, sharp incisors ready to clamp down on her throat.

“Kerrie, Kerrie, shhhh, it’s all right. I’m here.”

Kerrie fought the arms that held her. Another scream erupted from her lips. The grip around her body loosened.

“Kerrie, wake up. You’re having a nightmare. Kerrie.”

Dace laid a kiss on her wet forehead. More than anything, his lips brought her back to reality.

“Dace, I had this horrible nightmare. A bear—” She stopped in mid sentence as she realized that he sat on the bed beside her holding her in his arms. He wore a T-shirt and pajama pants.

“I was afraid of this. What about the bear?” His husky voice against her ear sent shivers down her spine. Dace pulled her tighter into his embrace.

"A bear attacked me. I thought it was just a bluff charge," she whispered against his chest. Dace caressed her hair soothingly. Kerrie pressed against him, listening to the beat of his heart. It seemed rather rapid. She inhaled his scent, a warm, woodsy, outdoor smell that curled her toes.

"I'm sorry, Kerrie. I think it was inevitable. You might have these nightmares for a while. That was a pretty horrendous experience you had this morning."

"You're telling me," Kerrie murmured against his chest. Against her better judgment, she pressed her lips softly against him, hoping the T-shirt would block the sensation. It was wrong. He belonged to someone else.

Dace seemed to stiffen for a moment, then resumed stroking her hair.

"How are you feeling now? Are you wide awake? Dream gone?"

"It's gone...for now." Kerrie wanted to prolong the moment in his arms as much as she could. He would surely push her away when he was ready. "How is it sleeping on the floor? Are you uncomfortable?" Kerrie heard a rumble in his chest as he chuckled.

"Yeah, I'm uncomfortable, but I don't think it has anything to do with the floor."

She grinned, thankful he could not see her expression against his chest. Moonlight continued to filter in, though the room seemed darker than before. Kerrie delighted in the anonymity of the darkness. No bright light exposed her naked desire, her willful and dishonest lust for a man not her own. She lay on his chest for a few more moments before she found the strength to move out of his arms.

But Dace did not release her. Instead, he found her face with his hand, lifted her chin and kissed her with a slow, lingering, silky kiss so sensual she couldn't have pulled herself away to save her life. She drifted away into the wonder of his mouth, lost on a sea of aching desire and rising passion.

Kerrie turned to press against his chest, and he enfolded her so tightly against him that a grain of sand could not have come between their bodies. Dace slid down the bed and matched her body's curves with his own. Kerrie lost all rational thought, knowing only that she wanted to lay in this man's arms forever. Forever.

Suddenly, Dace stiffened, and he lifted his head from hers. She reached to kiss his mouth again, but he held himself back, staring at her face in the soft moonlight. Kerrie couldn't see his expression. What happened?

"We can't do this, honey. Something's not right," Dace murmured in a voice roughened from ragged breathing. "A couple of hours ago, you told me I didn't have a chance with you. I doubt if anything has changed since then. You're probably just feeling scared right now and need some cuddling...which I'm happy to provide." He cleared the huskiness from his throat. "I just don't want to take advantage of that."

Kerrie went rigid. She thanked her lucky stars that at least *he* had come to his senses. Whatever attraction they had for each other would not survive infidelity.

"You're right, Dace. This is a terrible idea."

"Hey, sweetie, *I* didn't say this was a terrible idea. This is the best idea either one of us has had all day." His deep-throated chuckle shook her head as she lay against his chest. "I just think we have some stuff to work out first." Dace gave her a light kiss on the tip of her nose and hauled himself out of the bed. She stared up at him as he stood over her, grateful the darkness hid the burning color of her cheeks. "I'll be dreaming of you," he whispered, brushing her cheek with her fingertips before making his way across the room to return to his sleeping bag.

Kerrie rolled over, a single hot tear of reaction and humiliation escaping the corner of her eye. It seemed certain she would not be able to sleep after that encounter. She closed her thoughts against self-recrimination. What good would it do? She was in love. She could only hope to try to do the right thing and forgive herself when she strayed from her values. She set her jaw. That passionate kiss would not happen again. She would see to it.

****

Dace closed his eyes and waited for Kerrie's breathing to even out. Sometimes, she confused him so much he didn't know if he was coming or going. He held his breath as he listened to sounds of the night, the wind whistling through the trees, the odd call of a night owl, the sweet sounds of Kerrie's deep breathing.

He was proud of himself. It took every ounce of strength he had to pull away from her. He knew what he wanted, but Kerrie had been through a tough time, over the last few years, the last few months, and today. Tonight had not been the best night to take advantage of a frightened woman.

She'd told him no at dinner. He had no chance. But her responsive kiss said differently. He put his arms behind his head and stared at the moonlight filtering in the window. The woman drove him crazy. He knew he was in for a long and sleepless night. Mom's apple pie and baseball seemed too far away to be helpful in reducing his desire for the soft shape that lay in the bed across the room.

****

"So, how are you this morning, Sleeping Beauty?" Kerrie opened her eyes to the sight of Dace fully dressed, his sleeping bag rolled up and stowed onto his backpack. She rubbed her eyes, wondering how she'd managed to fall asleep after all.

Dace winked at her, but he kept his distance. Kerrie sighed and sat up in bed.

"I'm fine." She avoided meeting his eyes. He turned away as she rose from bed.

"I'm just going to wait outside while you get dressed." Dace grabbed his backpack and went out the door.

Kerrie shivered in the morning chill and quickly threw on a clean set of clothes. She laced up her boots with shaking fingers and grabbed her pack with a final search around the room for any stray belongings.

Dace leaned against the railing just outside the dormitory, his breath coming out in a cloud as he rubbed his hands briskly together.

"Boy, I can't wait for breakfast."

Kerrie gave him a shy smile and followed him down the trail. After a short stop at the restroom to wash up, they made their way into the dining room for a hearty breakfast of flapjacks.

Satiated by the delicious and hot food, Kerrie leaned back and patted her stomach. "I don't know how I'm going to make it back with all that food in me."

"I'll just fold you up in a ball and roll you down the hill. It's just a 3,300 foot decline. You should get back to Lake McDonald Lodge in no time at all." His deep throated chuckle warmed her heart.

She raised an eyebrow at him. "As long as I go faster than a speeding bear when we get to the huckleberry bushes, I'll be okay."

Dace grinned, but must have caught her failed attempt to hide her fear. He reached over and laid a warm hand on hers.

"We're going to be okay. I saw Bob last night...over by the campground. He said that he and Daniel tracked the bear for a few miles. It seemed well on its way to another huckleberry patch." A quick wink charmed her. "They posted signs of recent bear activity anyway though...just in case."

Kerrie channeled all her senses into the mesmerizing feel of his hand on hers, relished what would be his last touch if she had any say in the matter. And she did. She drew up her reserves and slipped her hand out from under his to reach for her glass of water.

Dace tilted his head inquiringly. He didn't miss much, but he said nothing.

The hike back down the mountain proved uneventful. They passed a few deer foraging in the forest along the way, but saw no sign of any bears. When they passed the huckleberry patch, Kerrie noticed the posted warning of recent bear activity. She also noticed that Dace moved protectively next to her. In such close proximity, she could smell his scent once again and she feared nothing.

At long last, they arrived at the parking lot of Lake McDonald Lodge. Kerrie's knees ached from the strain of the steep descent, and she longed to do nothing more than soak in a hot bath.

She parted from Dace with grateful thanks and an impersonal farewell, the ending of her grand adventure anticlimactic. In a fairy tale, he might have swept her off to a luxurious spa and slipped into a hot tub with her as she nursed her aching muscles, but that was not to be.

Two days later, Kerrie returned to work on her "Monday" to a notoriety she didn't foresee or want.

"Is it true you were bluff charged...by a grizzly?" James stared at her with unadulterated admiration and a new look of respect.

Kerrie turned abruptly, accidentally dropping her cash drawer.

"Where did you hear that?"

"Well, everyone knows about it. We heard Dace's call on the radio, and later Bob Hammond mentioned your name when he called in." James rubbed his junior ranger beard and continued to stare at her with awe. The tips of Kerrie's ears burned, as did her face. "So, what was it like?"

Kerrie shrugged her shoulders, ignoring the goose bumps that jumped up on her arms.

"What was what like?" Sandy sailed into the office. "Oh, hey there, bear bait. How are you doing after your ordeal the other day? I heard about it from Dace. Are you okay?"

The solicitous note in Sandy's voice almost brought Kerrie to tears. Guilt threatened to strike her dead. She swore it! Had Dace discussed *everything* with Sandy?

Kerrie moved to put her drawer away in the safe, casting a quick look at Sandy's face as she passed the stunning blonde woman. Sandy's beautiful blue eyes held nothing but friendly concern with their usual hint of humor.

"Hang on just a minute," Kerrie stalled while she stowed her drawer away. With no excuse left to avoid confrontation, she turned to the two rangers watching her curiously.

"It was horrendous. I was a big baby and I cried a lot, but the good new is I didn't wet my pants."

Sandy's and James' eyes flew open in shock before they burst into peals of laughter. Kerrie couldn't help laughing along with them, albeit her chuckles held a note of hysteria.

"That's always been my biggest concern too if I meet a bear in the woods, Kerrie." Sandy wiped the tears from her eyes. Small spurts of laughter continued to escape from her as she pressed the question.

"Other than dry pants though, are you all right? Dace said you were pretty shook up. He said you had nightmares. I imagine that's probably pretty normal. *I* know *I* would." Sandy continued to smile sympathetically.

Kerrie froze momentarily. Exactly what *had* Dace said?

"Uh, yeah, I did. Ummm..." What could she say?

Sandy moved near and gave Kerrie a quick hug. "I'll bet you did, poor thing." She dropped her arms, with a sympathetic tilt of her head in Kerrie's direction.

"Yeah, but what I want to know is how did it feel? Did you think you were going to die? Do you have time to think? How close did the bear get?"

"James, aren't you supposed to be heading out to the kiosk?" Sandy crossed her arms and gave him a stern look from under a raised brow.

James jumped and looked at his watch. "Dang, you're right. I'd better hustle. Okay, well, when you get a chance, Kerrie, I'd like to hear more about it." He grabbed his drawer and flew out the door, his hat permanently affixed to his head.

Thankful James couldn't continue to pester her, Kerrie dreaded the upcoming moment alone with Sandy. Would she now ask the hard questions about Dace? How much did she know? Escape seemed the wisest course at that moment.

"You know, I think I have to head for the outhouse." An unpleasant place to hide out, the nearby pit toilet was their only restroom facility.

"Okay, I'm going to head over after you."

Kerrie headed for the door, but not fast enough.

"Are you sure everything is okay, Kerrie? You look spooked. I don't blame you, of course."

Kerrie paused with a hand on the door. Caught! She turned to Sandy, unable to ignore the concern in her voice.

"Ummm...yeah, I am. I'm just stressed out, that's all."

"Well, from what Dace told me, you should be. Are you still having nightmares?"

"I didn't last night, but I watched TV until late, late, late just to make sure I'd sleep soundly." She bit her lip. She had to know. "Ummm...what did Dace tell you...about the nightmares?"

Sandy shrugged lightly. "Just that you woke up

screaming in the night. It's a good thing he was there. It's a *really* good thing he followed you up the trail to the chalet."

Kerrie's knees weakened. Sandy appeared to know everything. Well, almost everything.

"You...ah...you guys seem to have a pretty...mmm... open relationship." She cringed, squinting her eyes just a bit in case Sandy flew into an appropriate jealous rage.

Elegant, athletic shoulders shrugged once again. "Well, we're not joined at the hip or anything."

Just then the phone rang and Sandy turned away to grab it. Kerrie made good her escape.

When Kerrie returned after a prolonged delay of standing around the unpleasant outhouse and staring at the wooden walls, Sandy patted her on the back and headed into the woods herself. Kerrie busied herself with a few chores and saw an opportunity to escape when traffic built up in a line and she ran out to pass some cars through.

She came in half an hour later to find Sandy gone to lunch and Sam at work on the computer. He turned in his chair and surveyed Kerrie.

"So, you didn't take my advice."

Kerrie plopped into a chair and removed her hat, always heavier several hours into a shift. She shook her head ruefully.

"No, I didn't. I'm sorry."

Sam raised bushy, sandy eyebrows. "Oh, you don't need to apologize to me. You're the one who paid the price."

Kerrie stared hard at him, willing herself not to get angry at his righteous attitude.

"Besides, I'm the one who put Dace onto you." He crossed his arms with a smug smile.

"For goodness sake, Sam! Will you stop smirking? I made a mistake, and I'm not likely to make it again." She folded her own arms and fumed.

Sam dropped his arms. "Well, I know you're not, and I'm not smirking...much. I gotta tell ya though, I was pretty worried, and when I get worried, I get mad. That's a long hike to tackle on your own, especially for someone who has relatively little experience here at Glacier. I didn't know what to do about it, so I talked to Dace. Man, if you think I was worried, you should have seen his face. Furious would be a good word to describe it."

Kerrie swallowed hard and stared at Sam with wide eyes. "Really? He didn't seem mad when I saw him."

"Well, I guess not. If I hear tell right, seems you'd just been charged by a grizz." He shook his head. "Hardly the time for a lecture or a spanking."

Kerrie's eyebrows shot up. "A spanking? Oh, for Pete's sake, will the two of you stop treating me like a child? I was sheltered by my parents, not babied."

Sam's lips twitched, but he couldn't hold back a broad smile. He cleared his throat, but his voice continued to sound gruff.

"We just worry about you, Kerrie, that's all." He turned away to busy himself with some papers. Over his shoulder, she heard him say, "Dace sure seems to have a vested interest in your safety."

Kerrie peered around to see Sam's face, which bore a look of innocence she didn't buy for one minute.

"What does that mean?" she demanded.

"Nothing. I was just saying...that's all." He turned his attention to the computer where he began to work on the schedule.

"Sam." Kerrie's voice held a note of warning.

He turned back to her. "Just that I'm to tell him if you plan any more solitary hikes or if you get any strange phone calls or visitors here that upset you."

Kerrie jumped up. "That's none of his business, Sam. I appreciate the concern, but I think that's out of line." She stormed around the office while he placidly watched her.

"So, what's this about strange phone calls or visitors? Is there something I should know?"

Kerrie pace back and forth, gritting her teeth until her jaw ached. She was not a child to be mollycoddled. Just because it was nice to be taken care of once in a while, did not mean she couldn't take care of herself. Now! Kerrie knew without a doubt that she was not the same woman who once allowed a man to smack her around.

She paused for a moment, staring at Sam. "I ran away from an abusive relationship, and he's managed to find my phone number. I guess I'm a little worried he's going to find out where I am." She bit at her fingernail. "Okay, a lot worried. I confided in Dace the other night, but besides my folks, you two are the only ones who know."

"Geez, Kerrie, I didn't know. You poor kid."

Kerrie shook her head firmly, but she smiled. "No kid."

Sam raised his hands in mock defense. "Sorry, not a kid. Gotcha. It's hard to teach an old dog new tricks. Mary will tell you that."

Kerrie gave him a sympathetic grin. She knew he didn't mean to insult her.

"Well, listen, Sam, I've got to head out to relieve James. You won't tell anyone what I told you, will you?"

"No, Kerrie, I won't."

Kerrie retrieved her drawer and paused before she opened the door. She hoped she wasn't going to regret her next question, but she didn't know how to keep her mouth shut.

"Mmmm...Sam?"

"Yes?" he threw over his shoulder, deeply entrenched in the schedule facing him on the computer.

She drew in a deep breath. "About Dace?" Another breath. "Doesn't Sandy mind?"

"Mind what?"

She shifted from one foot to the other. "You know, how you say he has "a vested interest in my safety"."

Sam turned his head to peer at her. "I shouldn't see why. He *is* in law enforcement, after all."

"Oh," she replied, the wind taken out of her sales. He was, wasn't he?

"They're pretty close. She knows him pretty well," he mumbled as he turned back to the computer. He waved a hand in farewell. "See ya later."

Chapter Twelve

"Well, hi there. Long time no see," Deenie flashed her a fresh, young white-toothed smile. "I heard about your adventure. Are you all right?"

Kerrie almost jumped back from the counter. How could Deenie know?

"How did you know?"

"Oh, gosh, Kerrie! This is a small town. Everyone knows everything that goes on at Glacier. That Park is our pride and joy." She ran milk under the steamer for Kerrie's drink. "But not everyone gets charged by a bear. We've all seen them, gotten the heck out of their way, hoped they'd pass by peaceably, but I don't personally know anyone who's actually been that close to a grizzly."

Kerrie's hand shook slightly as she laid her money on the counter.

"I didn't know," she murmured.

"Yeah, Glacier is like our city park. What goes on at the Park does *not* stay at the Park." Deenie grinned as she made change. "Are you all right though?"

Kerrie nodded. "I'm fine. I was saved by a ranger, don't you know?" She hoped her tone sounded light and airy.

"Yeah, Dace." Deenie sighed. "That is one good looking hunk, isn't he? He could save me anytime."

Kerrie raised startled eyes to Deenie's laughing pansy brown eyes. "Well, he's too old for me, but if he weren't..." Deenie continued to grin.

Kerrie took her drink with an unsteady hand and gave Deenie a farewell wave. She grabbed a book on Yellowstone National Park from the travel section and made her way to a secluded seat to curl up and spend a comfortable hour dreaming of strange places, allowing the chocolate to boost her serotonin levels and improve her mood.

Two weeks had passed since her eventful hike to

Sperry Chalet, and she'd kept her feet on paved road and populated ground since. She had seen Dace only briefly as he'd driven through the gate in his patrol car. He occasionally stopped to ask how she was doing, but showed no rekindling of the intimacy they'd shared at the chalet. And for that, she was grateful. Kerrie had not seen him at the bookstore the last three times she had come.

James continued to pester her for details which she unwilling gave, knowing he was storing the information to fascinate fellow rangers and future visitors.

Sam kept a watchful eye on her, which she stopped resenting. Sandy grew somewhat preoccupied and secretive—an unexpected behavior for such an outgoing woman. She met Kerrie's eyes with an open expression, but she would leave at lunch and not discuss her destination. Ever alert, Kerrie saw her hop out of a truck one day that was not Dace's. She caught only a brief flash of a bearded ranger driving off. Sandy sauntered in from lunch, a frown on her face, and gave an evasive reply when Kerrie asked if anything were wrong.

Her mother reported no repeat sightings of Jack, and Kerrie received no more phone calls. It seemed Jack had gotten the message. All seemed right with the world, though Kerrie missed Dace terribly.

She flicked through the pages of the book on Yellowstone, noting they too had grizzly bears. Pictures of vast honey-colored plains dotted by herds of dark bison caught her eye. She found one especially entrancing, a photograph where several bison rolled on their backs near the hot mineral springs of a nearby geyser.

"Kerrie," a soft voice behind her chair sent a shiver down her spine. Kerrie began to shake uncontrollably. She swung around to see Jack standing above her.

Kerrie jumped up, the heavy book sliding to the floor with a loud bang.

"What are you doing here?" It was all she could do to keep from screaming. "How—"

Jack extended a hand to touch her, but Kerrie backed away.

"How did I find you?" He smiled, white teeth flashing across his handsome face, though his blonde good looks no longer held her in thrall. "Relax, Kerrie. Sit down. I'll pull up a chair and join you."

"No," she hissed. "No. You can't be here. You need to leave." Desperate eyes searched the bookstore for the comfort of knowing other people were around...and they were. Out of the corner of her eye, she saw several folks browsing books in nearby aisles.

"Kerrie, calm down. For Pete's sake, you'd think I was a serial killer or something. People are staring."

Kerrie had indeed caught a few inquiring glances, but she welcomed their curiosity. She also realized that she couldn't blindly rush out the door. What if Jack followed her...or worse yet, already knew where she lived?

"Don't tell me to calm down. How did you find me? Why are you here?" All the months of lonely seclusion, separated from her family and home, seemed wasted.

Jack ran a finger through the wavy golden hair that once reminded her of a surfer. His deceptively soft blue eyes scanned her face hesitantly. Kerrie was startled by the apparent vulnerability in his eyes. He'd always been so self-confident.

"You'd be surprised what one can find out on the Internet these days." He took a step in her direction, one hand held out beseechingly. "Please, Kerrie, can't we at least talk?"

Kerrie stared at him for a moment, the faint memory of a long forgotten love confusing her. Other memories flooded in and she crossed her arms and hugged herself.

"No, there's nothing to talk about. You had years to talk, but thought it was easier to get physical." Kerrie shivered at her defiance. She remembered a time when she had openly argued with him in public and paid dearly for it later. She planted her feet and stood her ground.

Jack dropped his head and shook it slowly. "I can't tell you how sorry I am for all those years, Kerrie. There is nothing I can do to fix what I did. I can't undo the past, though I wish I could." He shifted feet and glanced up at her from under veiled lashes. He smiled sheepishly. "I'm in a twelve-step program now, you know, for abusers." Jack winced slightly. "I hate that word."

"I do too," Kerrie boldly inserted.

"I'm on some mood stabilizing medication as well. I think it's working."

"That's good," Kerrie relented for a moment. Jack's submissive behavior threw her completely off guard, and she found her sympathies engaged against her better judgment.

"Step nine of the program requires that we make amends to those we have harmed. I'm trying to do that, Kerrie."

Jack regarded her steadily. Kerrie began to fidget, guilt nipping at her consciousness. The man looked genuinely remorseful. Maybe he had changed.

"Jack, I'm glad to hear that things are going well for you. I appreciate that you are trying to make amends. I just wish, though, that you had honored my request not to contact me. You already apologized over the phone. That was enough." Unable to make direct eye contact with him, a habit formed over years, she kept her eyes on his chin. A tremor passed through her body.

"I tried, Kerrie, but I needed to see you so much. I had to know you were okay. I was worried about you. You have to know that no matter how bad things got between us, I always loved you."

Kerrie once believed that to be true, but no longer. However, she chose to remain silent. Antagonizing him had been painful in the past.

Kerrie made a move to back up, but realized she didn't know if he had her home address.

"So, did the Internet give you my home address?" Kerrie bit her lip, hoping for an improbable answer. He must know where she lived.

Jack shook his head ruefully. "No, just the town. I've been here at the motel for a few days hoping to catch sight of you. I drove by here tonight on my way back to the room, and I saw your truck. The Washington license plate stood out amongst the Montana plates."

Kerrie could have kicked herself. But what could she have done? She had no way of knowing he would find her, no way of buying another car before she left...not without a job at the time.

"Kerrie, I was hoping—"

Kerrie swung around at the sound of Dace's voice. He paused in mid stride.

"Oh, excuse me. I didn't know you were talking to

someone." He gave Jack a friendly smile.

Kerrie's eyes flew back to Jack's face. Soft blue eyes hardened as he stared at Dace. In a flash, she knew all his efforts to change had failed. She watched in awe as the hardness disappeared in a flash and he extended a friendly hand toward Dace.

"The name's Jack. And you are?"

Dace stood stock still for a moment, suddenly narrowed eyes darting from Kerrie to Jack. He took Jack's hand in a brief shake.

"In law enforcement."

Jack's head reared and his eyes widened as he stared at his dark-haired counterpart. A muscle twitched his jaw and he gave a short laugh.

"Well, good for you," Jack murmured.

Dace put his hands on his hips in an expectant manner. Kerrie wished the ground would swallow her up. The last thing she needed was for Dace to meet Jack...or for Jack to meet Dace. Jack would know she had strong feelings for Dace. She could never hide anything from him.

For a moment, the two men stared at each other and Kerrie began to shake. She didn't want to stand in the middle. Instinct and experience drove her to protect her face, and she raised her hands to her cheeks in a disguised attempt to do so.

"Are you ready, Kerrie? We had plans tonight. Remember?"

To Kerrie's ears, Dace's voice seemed deeper than usual, his stature taller, his eyes harder.

"Kerrie, we have some things to discuss." Jack drew himself up and faced Dace, Kerrie seemingly forgotten in the middle.

She opened her mouth to speak, but no words came out.

"Kerrie? We'll be late. I've got reservations."

Kerrie stared at Dace. What was he talking about?

"I-I..."

"Kerrie, who is this? Are you dating a cop, for Pete's sake?" Irritation marred Jack's handsome face.

"Yeah, she is...not that I think it's any of your business."

Kerrie swung warning eyes to Dace who ignored her.

"No, Jack, I'm—"

"Yes, she is." Dace gave her a level gaze and then returned his belligerent stare to Jack. "So, if you'll excuse us, we have to be off." Dace put a gentle hand on Kerrie's back and guided her away from Jack and out the door. Kerrie dared not turn back to see Jack's face, but she could only imagine his thunderous rage.

Once outside, Kerrie turned to Dace.

"What are you doing?" she whispered urgently. "Don't make him angry."

"How did he find you? Did you tell him where you were? Did you call him?" Dace put his hands on his hips, emphasizing the accusing tone of his voice.

Kerrie sputtered. "Well, of all the—"

"It doesn't matter. We can't discuss it here. I don't think you should go home right now. Why don't you get in your truck and drive to the Keg. I'll follow you there...to make sure he doesn't follow." He looked over his shoulder and then back at Kerrie.

"Are you serious?" Angered by his insinuations, her first instinct was to refuse and return home. But she really didn't want to be alone at the moment, and she certainly didn't want Jack following her home. He would be likely to do just that.

She stalked off to her truck and Dace followed to his. As she began to pull out of the parking lot, she saw Jack come out of the building, and Dace turned back to approach him. Kerrie braked hard. She had every intention of intervening if fists started flying. A hysterical giggle escaped her lips. The image was ludicrous.

Kerrie held her breath and watched. Dace strode up to Jack and the two men exchanged words. Though Kerrie could not hear the conversation, the exaggerated gesticulations by Jack answered by Dace's menacing rigid posture told her all she needed to know. Within minutes, Jack turned and stormed off toward his car. Kerrie saw that it was a sports car, the same model as his red vehicle in Washington, but the color was white. Specific Montana tags indicated it was a rental. He must have flown in.

Then she gripped the steering wheel and stared hard at the car again. A white sports model followed her two weeks ago...or so she had thought. She shook her head as Jack peeled out of the parking lot with all the appearance of a very angry man. It couldn't have been Jack. Her mother had seen him the day prior in Washington.

Dace got into his truck and pulled up behind her. Kerrie drove slowly out of the parking lot, keeping an eye on Dace in the rear. When they arrived at the restaurant, Kerrie climbed gingerly out of her vehicle and waited for Dace.

"What was that all about?"

"I'll tell you when we get inside." Dace put a hand lightly behind her back and guided her into the restaurant.

"Listen, Dace, I'm all right now. You don't have to...and I'm beginning to hate this word, but...babysit me."

He gave her a sly grin. "Of course, I don't."

Kerrie narrowed his eyes at his unanswerable reply.

"Hi ya'll." Sally bustled forward with menus in hand. "Is a booth all right?"

"Sounds good, Sally," Dace murmured.

"I heard about your bear encounter," Sally threw over her shoulder as they followed her to a table. "Must have given you quite a scare. My husband ran into a grizzly once himself. Nothing much happened, but I had the dickens washing his pants out after that."

Caught off guard, Kerrie burst into nervous laughter. Dace chuckled.

"Sally, you sure are a salty woman, aren't you?"

The stout red-head grinned. "I'm just telling it like it is." She buzzed away, leaving a grinning Kerrie and Dace with two menus.

Kerrie looked at Dace and her smile faded. "So, what happened at the bookstore?"

Dace stared hard at her for a moment. "I might ask you the same question. So, you didn't call him or let him know where you were? Did you *want* him to come here? I had the impression you didn't?"

Kerrie's cheeks flamed. "No," she said hotly. "I didn't call him. He says he found out where I was on the Internet and I believe him. It's ridiculous how much private information gets posted out there." She shook her head angrily. "I don't know how he got here, and I'm beginning to wonder if he hasn't been here for a while."

Kerrie told Dace about the night she thought she'd been followed, but that her mother had seen Jack in Washington.

Dace gritted his teeth, his blue-gray eyes darkened to slate. "Why didn't you tell me?"

Kerrie shrugged. "I don't know. The next day was the Sperry Chalet hike so you can imagine that the car slipped my mind." She bit her lip and met his eyes squarely. "Besides, I can't come running to you for every little thing. I don't know you that well."

Dace tilted his head, a trait she had come to love. "Yes, you do." He didn't explain.

Kerry shied from the intimate insinuation. "Are you going to tell me what went on at the bookstore?"

"Well, you haven't explained what he wanted, but my best guess is he wants you back or something like that."

Kerrie's eyes dropped to her menu, but she didn't reply.

"I told him to stay away from you. I told him I know about the restraining order in Washington and that if he didn't think it wouldn't be enforced in Montana, he was mistaken."

A tremor ran through Kerrie. She peeked up at Dace whose stern face intimidated even her at the moment.

"And?"

"And what?"

"Well, that was a long conversation for such a short replay. What did Jack say?"

Dace gazed at her steadily. "Nothing of substance. I think he'll head out. I told him to be out of town by sunrise."

Kerrie's eyes widened. "Can you actually say that?"

Dace's lips twitched, a twinkle danced in his softening eyes. He shrugged. "I did. I'll have the local police check on him in the morning, but I kind of liked that *sunrise* bit."

Kerrie shook her head, a smile playing on her lips. "You're such a cowboy."

Dace laughed. Sally returned to take their orders, and with no time to actually review the menu, Kerrie ordered the same food she'd had the last time.

"How have you been over the last few weeks?" Dace asked in a soft, embracing voice.

Kerrie steeled herself against his insistent charm.

"Fine," she replied, trying to keep her tone brief and no-nonsense.

Dace nodded. "I noticed a book by your feet at the bookstore, a book on Yellowstone." He paused for a moment and stared at the thumbs of his clasped hands. "Are you thinking about going there?"

Kerrie thought she would surely drown in the molten silver of his eyes. She tried to focus on the innocuous questions.

"Yellowstone?" she murmured inconsequentially. "I-I don't think so." Pulling herself out of the hypnotic depth of his gaze, she focused more clearly. The book on Yellowstone...the pictures. Steaming hot springs, towering geysers, silky water in multicolored travertines, sweeping panoramas of herds of chocolate brown bison with taffy brown babes at their sides. Hardly aware that she sighed, Kerrie spoke.

"Well, maybe. I'm not sure. I don't remember much about the trip we took when I was little. It's beautiful, isn't it?"

Dace nodded, his eyes intently studying her face. "It is. I worked there a few years ago, but I wasn't there very long."

Kerrie blinked at his searching gaze. "Do I have something on my face? You're staring." She self-consciously wiped the corner of her mouth. Perhaps a spittle of saliva left over from her recent encounter with Jack?

Dace widened his eyes and pulled back slightly. "Was I? Sorry. Just thinking."

"About what?" She looked down at his laced fingers where he pushed his thumbs against each other to the point they turned white. Was something wrong?

"It's funny you should be reading that book on Yellowstone." He gave her a lopsided grin. "I...uh...I applied for a job there. Heard today that I got accepted."

Kerrie's heart plummeted. She stopped breathing for a moment...or two. "Yellowstone?" A thousand questions assaulted her brain, begging to escape her lips. She bit down hard against them and looked away toward the bustling restaurant as she tried to figure out an appropriate response.

"Kerrie?"

She swung her eyes back toward his, unable to decipher the question in his eyes.

"Well, congratulations, Dace. When do you leave? Next summer?" Her heart pleaded for an answer she could live with.

"No, I have to be there in August, a few weeks from now."

"Oh, no." The words escaped Kerrie's lips against her will. "I mean, wow, that's sudden. I had no idea."

"I've been thinking about it for a while. I only stayed there one year before they needed me up here, and I'd like to spend some more time down there."

"What about..." Her eyes darted to his face and down to the red checkered tablecloth.

"What about?"

"Umm...Sandy? What does she think about this? Is she going?"

Dace knitted his brows together. "I don't know what's going on with her. She's...she's become secretive lately."

Kerrie cringed. Had Sandy found out about the kiss? Kerrie took a deep breath.

"Do you think she knows? Did you tell her about...you know...the kiss that night?"

Dace studied Kerrie's face for a long time...too long for her comfort. He smiled softly and shook his head. "No, I didn't."

"Oh," seemed a weak response, but nothing else came to mind. Did Sandy suspect that Kerrie had fallen in love with her man? A memory came unbidden. The blur of a ranger's face as he drove out the exit after dropping Sandy off at the gate. Was Sandy seeing someone else?

Their food arrived and the next few minutes were preoccupied with Sally's attentions. Not unexpectedly, Kerrie had no appetite, and she toyed with her food. She noticed that Dace hardly ate himself.

"Have you thought about where you plan to work next season? *Are* you returning to the Park next year or are you heading home? I guess the reason for hiding out here is...moot at this point anyway. What are your plans?"

Kerrie could hardly absorb the impact of Dace's departure much less her own future plans. What would she do?

"I don't know." She stopped pretending to eat and put down her fork. "I really don't know. I'd like to go home and see my family and my dog." She shook her head slightly as she stared at a distant spot over his shoulder. "I don't want to be in a place where Jack can continue to find me though. The restraining order is not deterring him very much."

"Well, you haven't called the police to enforce it, have you?"

Kerrie hung her head for a moment. "No, I haven't. I know I should. I just hate to see him go to jail."

"From the anger I saw in his eyes tonight, I think that's where he belongs. I'm worried about you, Kerrie."

Kerrie gave him a small smile. If he was worried about her, why didn't he stay with her?

"I'll be all right, Dace. Really. If he tries to contact me again here or back in Washington, I'll call the police."

"Good. So, you're returning to Washington?" He cleared his throat.

Kerrie nodded. "At least to see my parents. I don't know where I'm going this winter or if I'll return to the Park Service next season."

"Sam will hire you again in a heartbeat. He says you're a fine worker."

Kerrie blushed. "Sam... Between the two of you, I've got more nursemaids than a gal knows what to do with."

Dace grinned. "You can never have enough, love."

Kerrie's startled eyes flew to his. A strange light danced in the swirling depths of cobalt blue. "Love?"

"Oh, yeah," he replied firmly.

"So, are you ready for the check?" Sally swung by the table with paper in hand, putting a temporary stop to any further words.

Dace nodded and reached for his wallet. Kerrie stared at him dumbfounded, but he busied himself with their departure, declining her offer to pay for the meal. She preceded him out the door as he held it open for her.

"Now, listen. I'm going to follow you home...and I'm

going to wait for a few minutes after you get inside...just to make sure Jack hasn't found your home address."

Kerrie sighed. "Dace, I can't tell you how embarrassed I feel about you going out of your way to watch over me."

"If I don't do it, Sam is going to. I had to beat him to it. He made me promise to keep an eye on you."

Kerrie grinned. "Sam," she murmured affectionately. "That guy."

"He's a great guy."

"Yes, he is." With a quick scan of the parking lot, she climbed into the truck. Dace closed the door for her, climbed into his own vehicle, and followed her out of the parking lot.

Kerrie kept a watchful eye on parked cars, stray headlights, and dark alleys, but she didn't see Jack's white sports car anywhere. His car wasn't parked at the motel, and she hoped he'd had the sense to leave town...as Dace put it.

She pulled into the quiet parking lot of her apartment building. Dace pulled into a spot next to her and waited. Kerrie stopped by his truck.

"Good night, Dace. Thanks for everything. It seems like I'm always thanking you for rescuing me."

She could see the flash of his teeth as he smiled, though no moon helped to light the night. It took all her willpower not to beg Dace to come upstairs, to stay with her through the night...and the next night and the one after that.

"Don't worry about it, Kerrie." Another quick grin. "Like I said, Sam will kill me if I don't watch over you...or he'll drag Mary out of bed for an all-night stakeout. She'd do it, too. She's up for anything."

Kerrie shook her head ruefully, glad he couldn't see her red cheeks. She made her way upstairs and stepped into her apartment. A quick flip of the switch indicated all was well. The apartment seemed untouched, and she turned in the doorway to wave at Dace in the parking lot before she closed and locked the door.

Kerrie leaned on the door, fighting the continuing urge to beg him to stay. She didn't fear being alone that night so much as she did losing him in a few weeks when he left for Yellowstone. She felt empty already as she imagined Glacier National Park without his presence. He had become her rock, the lighthouse that guided her in the dark, the reason she jumped out of bed every morning. She couldn't bear the thought of his departure and wondered bleakly what he would think if she wandered into Yellowstone next year as a seasonal employee. She doused herself with a splash of cold reality as she reminded herself—what would Sandy and he think if she wandered into Yellowstone next year?

Kerrie turned away from the door and headed for the bathroom to take a hot shower. She undressed and stepped in, letting the steaming water envelop her in a caressing embrace. The image of Dace's face swam before her eyes as she soaped up. She dreamed of being in his arms in a hot mineral spa...somewhere in Yellowstone. Finding herself more stimulated than relaxed, she shook her head with a mischievous grin and turned off the water. As she stepped out of the shower, she heard the ringing of her phone. Grabbing a towel, she ran for the living room to find her purse. It was Dace.

"Hello?" Her heart quickened in anticipation of hearing his voice. Had he somehow heard her sensual thoughts in the shower? Was he volunteering to come upstairs?

"Hello, Kerrie."

Kerrie pulled the phone away from her ear and stared at it in horror. Caller ID showed D. Mitchell, but the voice was Jack's.

"Jack," she whispered. "What are you doing? How did you get Dace's phone?"

"Well, I have his phone because I took it off him. He's sitting here in his truck with a knot on the front of his head that's going to hurt a lot when he wakes up...*if* he wakes up."

If he wakes up. A cold chill seized Kerrie's heart. Black swirls swam before her eyes. She dropped weakly onto the couch, the phone pressed hard against her ear.

"Jack, please, don't hurt him. What did you do? Oh, please, tell me you didn't kill him?"

"No, I don't think I did. But here's the thing, Kerrie." His horrible voice took on a conversational tone. "If you don't let me in your apartment, I *am* going to kill him. I've got a tire iron here, and I have no problem hitting him over the head with it. I already did once."

Kerrie heard his voice through a fog of shock. His words seemed clear, but they made no sense. She fought hard to stay conscious, forcing herself to take in a breath...at least one. She choked off a wave of nausea.

"I-I...what are you doing?" she whispered in a ragged voice. Kerrie dragged herself off the couch and approached the window. Afraid of what she might find, she lifted the corner of one small blind.

In the faint light of the late moon, she could see Jack standing by Dace's truck. He waved a menacing tire iron in one hand and held the phone to his ear with the other.

"Do you want to see me take a practice swing? Open the door and stay on the phone until I get up there. I don't want you calling the police."

"Please don't hurt him, Jack. He's just a co-worker."

"Oh, I think he's a bit more than that, to hear him tell it, Kerrie. Let me in."

Kerrie saw no other choice. Even through all the years of violence, she'd never heard his voice so taut, so threatening.

"Okay, okay." Kerrie moved to the door and pulled it open. She wore only a towel around her unclothed body, but could not take time to get dressed.

"Stay on the phone."

"I'm here."

Jack moved away from Dace's truck and bounded across the parking lot and up the stairs. Kerrie backed into her living room as he neared. He stepped in and shut the door behind him, pausing only to lock it. He dropped the phone on the floor and snatched Kerrie's cell phone out of her hand to toss it across the room. The tire iron dangled from his hand.

Kerrie froze in the middle of the living room, assuming a posture she'd practiced for three years—guarded stillness, eyes cast down on the floor with his feet in sight, face neutral, arms in an undefended position at her sides. Much like one should posture when facing a grizzly bear...submissive.

"Well, looks like you were expecting some good times

tonight. Did I interrupt something?"

Kerrie kept her eyes on the floor. "No, Jack. Dace was worried and wanted to wait in the parking lot."

"Oh, really?" he mocked. A mild maniacal pitch in his voice made her cringe. She hadn't heard that note before. One could defend against the known terror...but not the unknown.

"And what was Dace so worried about? Me? What lies have you told him, Kerrie?"

"Nothing," she mumbled.

"Liar," he taunted.

Kerrie kept her eyes on his feet, occasionally peeking at the tire iron in his hand. She knew he wanted her to argue, to fight back. That always incited him more. He had little incentive to strike if she did not move or speak.

"You know, I came here a few weeks ago looking for you, Kerrie, but I had to get back to Washington for my counselor's appointment. Can't miss that now, can I? What with getting better and all. I thought I found you one night, but..." Jack's voice hardened. "It was you, wasn't it? You saw my car, didn't you, and you hid?"

Kerrie nodded, just a slight movement of her head.

A palpable quiet deafened the room. She held her breath. What was coming?

"Drop your towel."

Kerrie's pounding heart seemed to stop. Oh no! Jack had never done anything like that. Please no.

"Drop your towel, Kerrie. Let me see what Dace was looking forward to."

Kerrie ground her feet further into the carpet with a thought toward launching herself in an effort to flee. Jack found her breaking point. He almost always did.

"No, Jack."

"What do you mean...no?" Jack stepped forward and reached for her. He grabbed the towel as she made her move. In a flash, she ran for the bedroom, but Jack lunged and caught her as she fled through the door. He dropped the tire iron and threw her on the bed, his hands heading for her throat. Kerrie struggled against his grip, pulling at his fingers as blackness threatened to engulf her.

"I'm going to kill you, I swear it," Jack snarled.

Though she tried to scream, no sounds came from her

choked throat. Jack's face swam above hers, red with glittering eyes and bared teeth. The grizzly bear had attacked at last.

Chapter Thirteen

Through the deafening sound of blood pounding in her ears, she heard a loud crash, a shout, and a sea of voices as Jack slumped over her body. Though his grip on her throat lessened, she thought she would pass out from his dead weight on her chest. Male voices penetrated the roaring in her ears.

"Get him off her, for Pete's sake."

"Dispatch, we need a forensics unit out here."

"Kerrie! Kerrie, honey, are you all right?" A husky voice prodded her consciousness. "Get him out of here. Let me cover her up."

Someone pulled Jack off her and she clutched the bedspread for cover.

"Here, sweetie, here, I'm going to cover you up."

"Dispatch, is that ambulance on its way? Dace, you need to get that head looked at."

"Forget about me. I want them to take a look at her." The voice grew somber. "Kerrie, I'm sorry, I'm so sorry I didn't take better care of you."

Kerrie felt herself wrapped up in a blanket like a little burrito. For some reason, her vision was clouded, but she could see that Dace sat on the bed holding her, occasionally reaching to tuck in a spare corner of the cover. Several uniformed officers kept a watchful eye on Jack's slumped figure by the door. A strange man surveyed Kerrie and Dace while he spoke on a cell phone.

Kerrie looked up at Dace's grave face. A one-inch gash on the left side of his forehead marked the spot where Jack had hit him. She thanked everything she could think of that Dace survived the assault.

"Dace, I'm sorry. I'm so sorry."

"Well, you're both a sorry pair, apparently. Enough of that nonsense now. Are you well enough to tell us what happened, young lady?"

Dace looked over her shoulder at the man in street

clothes. "Come on now, Jim. She's been through enough, and my head is killing me. I'll come down to the station in about half an hour and make a statement. You've got enough info to get your report going. Okay?" He glanced at Jack's unconscious body. "Just take him out of here. This guy needs to go to prison."

Kerrie followed his eyes and shuddered. Prison. It seemed so hard. How could someone she once loved go to prison?

Jim eyed them thoughtfully. "Are you all right with him here, miss?" He nodded in Dace's direction. "Do you want a female officer here?"

Kerrie nodded her head. She tried to say no to the second offer, but her aching throat gave up no sounds. She shook her head.

Jim smiled kindly. "I'll take that as a yes, he can stay, and no, you don't need a female officer. I think you'll probably spend the night in the hospital anyway."

Kerrie stiffened and stared at Jack's form. Even to her befuddled brain, it seemed likely that Jack would end up in the hospital. Someone must have knocked him out, and he would need to be examined for concussion. She didn't want to be in the same building as he.

Dace held her close. "Don't worry. I'm going to be right there with you."

Kerrie heard the tenderness in his voice before she lost consciousness.

****

She awoke to the warmth of a warm, protective palm covering her left hand. Her right hand felt cold, and she looked down drowsily to see an IV pressed into it. With a start, she realized she was in the hospital. Where was Jack? She jerked involuntarily, her eyes darting to Dace as he sat in a chair by her bed, his head resting against the hand that he held, eyelashes lying against drawn cheeks. Unwilling to wake him, she gazed at his shining dark locks. A bandage on his forehead covered his wound. She hoped his injury wasn't too severe.

She longed to remove her hand from under his and run her fingers through his silky hair. He seemed quite, quite asleep and she thought she might try. She eased her hand out carefully.

"Well, here you are." Sandy breezed into the room and stopped in her tracks. "Wow, he's passed out. Is he all right?"

Kerrie's eyes bulged as Sandy moved quickly toward Dace. She peered over to look at the bandage on his forehead. Dace's eyes fluttered open and he saw Sandy. He bolted upright, only to grab the front of his head.

"Man, that hurts," he muttered.

"I'll bet. I heard about what happened. Sam called me." Sandy's eyes passed between Kerrie and Dace, her brow knotted.

Dace turned a concerned eye toward Kerrie. She tucked her left hand under her hip and gave him a smile, though an uncontrollable tremor caught the left side of her lips.

"Sorry. I must have passed out. Are you all right?" Dace leaned in to study Kerrie's face.

She opened her mouth to speak, to urge him not to stay, but a rasp was the only sound to escape her lips. She put a quick hand to her throat.

Dace turned toward Sandy. "I don't think she can talk right now." He returned his gaze to Kerrie. "The doctor said you'll be all right in a day or two."

Kerrie nodded, though the motion hurt her neck.

"What happened?" Sandy ran a tender hand along Dace's hairline, careful to avoid the bandaged area. He pulled her hand to his lips, kissed the back briefly and then released it.

Kerrie winced at the sight, and with no escape available, she closed her eyes against the couple, pretending to drowse.

She heard Dace rise from the chair. "Let's step out. She needs to sleep." He lowered his voice to a whisper.

"Are you okay? Sam said you got hit with a tire iron? What the heck has been going on?" Sandy's whisper carried a strident note of confusion and anxiety.

"Shhh. I'll explain it all. Let's go down to the cafeteria."

The muffled swish of the door signaled their departure and Kerrie opened her eyes once again. Hot tears spilled out the corners and ran down the sides of her face. She quickly mopped them up with her free hand, angry with her foolish blubbering. This was a fine time for Sandy to appear, she thought. Truly. It seemed fitting that Sandy should charge in, solidifying her place in Dace's life. *She* was the woman who should touch his hair. *She* was the woman who would tend to his wounds. And the sooner he left for Yellowstone, the better off Kerrie would be.

She closed her eyes again and, with the help of whatever magic potion dripped through her IV, thankfully fell asleep to the comforting clinks, clanks, and bustle of a busy hospital.

"Kerrie? Kerrie." Kerrie opened reluctant eyes and met Dace's soft blue-gray gaze as he stood beside her bed. She looked behind him, but did not see Sandy.

Dace gave her a gentle smile and sat down in the chair beside her bed. He reached for her free hand, but she had the presence of mind to tuck it up under her hip once again. He searched her face with a quizzical expression, sighed and settled back into the chair.

"You slept all night. Did you eat breakfast?"

Kerrie's eyes widened and she searched the room for a clock.

"It's almost eleven."

Kerrie shook her head. "Really?" she rasped, her throat painfully raw.

"Yeah. The nurses said you slept all night and half the morning. I came back to the room to see you again last night, but you seemed comfortable, so I went home for a shower."

"How's your head?" she whispered.

He gingerly touched his forehead. "I'll live. Twenty stitches. No concussion."

Kerrie gritted her teeth against the onslaught of guilt. "I'm so sorry."

Dace leaned forward with an intent expression. "Don't be, honey. It's not your fault. *You* didn't hit me." He shook his head ruefully, then winced at the motion. "Ouch." He leaned back in his seat once again. "I just can't believe I let him get the slip on me. I was supposed to be watching out for you. And I failed miserably."

Kerrie's heart melted at the angry look on Dace's face.

“I’m madder at myself than him.”

“Don’t be, Dace.” She struggled to whisper and reached for a cup of water by the bed. Dace rose to help her drink, then put the cup back down.

“Well, I am. Nothing is going to change that. He’s in jail now though. They’re going to charge him with assault with a deadly weapon and attempted murder. He’s going away for a long time.” A grim expression matched the gravity of his voice.

“I can’t believe it. Poor Jack.”

“You’re not feeling sorry for him, are you, Kerrie?”

Kerrie nodded carefully, her neck still sore. “I do feel sorry for him. Sorry and guilty. Sorry for someone I used to love and guilty for just about everything...including that gash on your head.”

Dace stared hard at her for a moment, but his eyes softened. “Yeah. I can imagine. Nothing is black and white, is it?” He sighed. “He belongs in prison though, Kerrie. You know that, don’t you?”

“I know he needs to be locked away somewhere. If he really was getting therapy, it’s not helping.”

“I don’t think so.”

Kerrie nodded. “What happened? How did the police get there?”

“Well, I called them after you went upstairs. I just wasn’t sure about Jack. I asked them to have a patrol stop by.” Dace grinned. “It’s a small town. The Chief of Police, Jim, heard the call and decided to swing by as well. In fact, he got there first and slapped me around a bit until I woke up.” The twinkle in his eye belied his words. “Anyway, we all charged upstairs. They busted down the door and I returned Jack’s love tap on the back of his head.” Dace grimaced. “When I saw him on top of you with his hands around your neck...” He swallowed hard. “I thought we were too late.” Kerrie watched the muscle of his jaw flex as he stared at a distant point over her head.

“I’m okay,” she whispered.

Dace returned his gaze to her face. He leaned forward. “Yes, you are.”

Kerrie blinked against the intensity in his eyes.

He relaxed and took a deep breath. “Listen, Kerrie. Sam told me to tell you to take a week off, more if you need it. He thought you might like to go home for a while."

Kerrie stared at the face of the man she loved, knowing that she was gazing at him for the last time. She nodded.

"That sounds like a good idea," she murmured. "I do need to go home. You'll be gone when I get back." The flat statement sounded like a death toll to Kerrie's ears.

Dace nodded. "Yeah, I'm due in Yellowstone by the end of next week. Kerrie, I was wondering..."

"Dace, thank you so much for everything. I wish you good luck down there. It's just the funniest thing. I still feel so tired. I think I need to get some sleep."

Kerrie closed her eyes against Dace's beloved face and forced herself to breathe evenly as if she were indeed asleep. She didn't hear the door open for the longest time, but dared not peek to see if he was still there. Mercifully, the medications kicked in and she fell asleep within minutes.

Dace stared at Kerrie's pale face for a while. He couldn't bear to leave her this vulnerable, but he had to go. Soon, her parents would come to take her home. Would she return to Glacier? Would she hang up her ranger hat and remain there in Washington in the town she'd known all her life?

"How's she doing?" the nurse whispered over his shoulder.

"Fine, I guess. Sleeping a lot," he smiled at the older woman who checked Kerrie's IV.

"Yeah, that's because she's getting something to help her relax. We want her to sleep for a while." She paused at the door as she left. "Her parents are here. They're talking to the doctor right now. I'm going to send them in shortly."

"Okay, good," Dace whispered. "Hey, do you have some paper and an envelope I can borrow?"

"I'll get some."

Dace turned back to Kerrie. He touched the hand she'd tucked so protectively under her hip. Her parents would probably take her home soon. Was this the last time he would ever see her?

A painful knot formed in his throat. He swallowed

against it, but the pain intensified and moved down into his chest.

He hoped not. He leaned forward and kissed the back of her hand. He couldn't bear it if he didn't see her again. Would she come to him? Could she leave everything she'd ever known and come to him?

****

"Kerrie? Honey?" A familiar voice awakened her.

"Mom," she croaked, eyeing the anxious figure of her mother as she hovered over the bed. Her father stood by the opposite side of the bed, a grave look on his quiet face.

"Oh, honey. How do you feel? Are you okay?"

"How did you guys get here?"

"A fellow named Dace Mitchell called us. Said he was a park ranger and a friend of yours. He told us what happened."

Kerrie shook her head, though it hurt to do so. The interfering man! How she loved his meddling ways. Would he never go away?

Her mother thrust an envelope in her hand. "Here, this was on your bed tray. It's for you."

Kerry took the plain white business envelope in her hand and eyed it curiously. Her name was handwritten on the front. She set it aside on the bed under the barrage of her mother's questions.

"I can't believe Jack. Are you all right? What happened? I know a little bit, but Dace was somewhat reticent about giving out a lot more than just telling us Jack had tracked you down, attacked you and was now in jail."

Her mother put a dramatic hand to her ample chest. "I can't tell you how angry I am. I hate him." Venom dripped from her lips as she plunked down into the nearby beside chair.

Her mother opened her mouth to speak again. "Daddy, talk to her. I'm biting my lip right now."

Kerrie turned bemused eyes on her father who stood by uncertainly. He laid a gentle hand on his daughter's forehead. "I'm so sorry this happened, Kerrie." His gruff voice reassured her.

Kerrie grabbed her father's hand and laid it against her cheek for a brief moment, which was all the demonstrative affection she thought he could handle.

"Thanks, Dad."

Kerrie turned to her mother. "Did you drive over?"

"Yes, we did, took off in the middle of the night to get here. Your friend, Dace—who seems to know everything by the way—said that your boss has given you some time off. So, if you don't mind coming home to see Suzie, I'll drive back home with you, and Dad will follow us in the car."

Kerrie's head whirled. Things were happening fast. She felt a wave of nausea as she imagined driving away from Montana...away from Dace.

"I-I...that sounds fine, Mom. When do I get out of the hospital?"

"The doctor says you can leave in an hour. We just have to keep an eye on you to make sure there's no drowsiness from the pain medication they've been giving you."

"An hour! Well, when were you planning on returning?"

"As soon as we leave, honey. It's about a six hour drive, and we've got plenty of daylight left. I stopped by your place and grabbed your purse and a few things."

Kerrie caught her breath. Leave the place where Dace lived and breathed? In an hour? Did she have the strength?

Through the partially open doorway, she caught sight of a blonde nurse, her luxurious ponytail swaying as she moved past with a cart. Sandy had a similar head of shiny hair.

Kerrie returned her gaze back to the faces of her beloved parents. Yes, she could leave Montana in an hour. And when she returned to fulfill her contract, Dace would be gone...and most likely Sandy with him.

****

Kerrie ruffled Suzie's curls as the little dog lounged in her lap.

"Why do you have to go back, honey? They'll understand if you break the contract. Although I think that term sounds awfully rough."

"Mom, I have to go back. I'm sure they'll understand if I don't feel I can return, but I know I can. Jack is in jail without bail. There is nothing more to fear."

"Exactly!" Her mother bustled about the kitchen preparing dinner. "So, why can't you stay here?"

"Because I need to go back. I want to go back. I didn't really say goodbye to the Park. You don't just walk away from a park like that without a farewell."

Her mom stopped peeling potatoes and turned to survey her daughter.

"Who are you? You've changed so much this summer, I hardly recognize you. It took you years to find the courage to leave town...and Jack...and now here you are ready to fly off again."

Kerrie chuckled and hugged Suzie. "I know. Bizarre, isn't it?"

"Are you coming home after the contract is over in October?" She dropped the peeled potatoes in a pot. "I miss you. We miss you."

Kerrie set the dog down on the floor and stood up to slip her arms around her mother's soft waist. She laid her head on her mother's back.

"I miss you guys too, but I don't think I'm going to make a life here, Mom. The town is awfully small." She raised her arms expansively. "There's a whole world out there just calling to me."

Suzie jumped up and down, barking in enthusiasm at the high pitch in Kerrie's voice.

Kerrie chuckled and scooped the dog up in her arms. "No, you don't get to go...not yet. Let's just wait and see where I end up. I don't know if Dad can do without you, sister."

"Sister is right." Kerrie's mom wiped her hands on a dishtowel. "Your dad treats her like a child. She jumps onto his lap anytime he sits down. He dotes on her."

"That settles it then. At least she stays."

Kerrie's cell phone rang, and she glanced at it on the table. The caller ID said "D. Mitchell." She turned away and walked over to stare out the sliding glass door leading to the back yard.

"Is that Dace again?"

Kerrie nodded.

"Why aren't you taking his calls, honey? He seemed like such a nice man. If I heard the story correctly, you owe him your life."

A shudder passed through Kerrie's body. She bit her lip.

"I do owe him my life, Mom. There's no doubt about that. I'm pretty sure Jack was going to kill me."

"So, why won't you take his calls? How many times has he called over the last couple weeks?"

"Fourteen," Kerrie murmured. "Once a day since I left."

"Well, have you listened to the messages? Maybe it's something from work?"

Kerrie shook her head. "No, I haven't listened to the messages...if there are any. Anyway, it's not work. I talked to my boss, Sam, and he would have told me any work-related news."

"Kerrie, the only reasons a woman won't take a call from a handsome man are because she can't stand him or she's in love. Which is it?"

Kerrie turned and surveyed her short, dark-haired mother with a rueful smile. "It's not that I can't stand him."

Her mom dropped into a seat. "Kerrie! Then why won't you talk to him. Believe me, child, I saw him. I can't imagine one reason why you wouldn't be calling him."

"He's already involved with another woman, a co-worker of mine. I think they've been together for a couple of years."

The older woman's face drooped. "Oh dear, I see. Yes, well, I can certainly understand."

"Mmm hmmm."

"Well, I'm sure he's just calling to see how you're doing."

"I'm sure he is."

Kerrie's mother sighed. "So, when are you leaving?"

"First thing in the morning, Mom. I'm supposed to work day after tomorrow."

"I'm going to miss you, honey."

"I'll miss you guys, too, Mom, but at least I know I can come home when I want now."

****

Kerrie put a determined smile on her face and strode up to the office, adjusting her ranger hat along the way.

The cool morning temperature heralded the arrival of an Indian summer with fall just around the corner. Already, the leaves of the surrounding trees and bushes blazed in colors of orange and yellow in preparation for what promised to be a spectacular autumn show.

James stepped out of the office and strode up to her. He barred her way.

"Kerrie. I feel so bad about what happened. I-I think I'm the one who gave that guy your phone number."

Kerrie reared back to stare at the troubled young man. His beard had thickened over the summer.

"What do you mean?"

"Back in June, someone called...a man. He said he was with Human Resources, you know...personnel, and that he wanted to verify your phone number. The number he gave me was completely off, and I gave him the correct one...the one we had on file here."

Kerrie softened at the look of utter misery in James' eyes. "Wow! That was pretty creative of Jack. That's probably how he figured out where I worked. He must have called a dozen national parks looking for me. He knew I'd always wondered about working at the Park." She laid a reassuring hand on James' arm. "It's okay, James. He found my address through the Internet."

"Yeah, but he found you here in Montana because of me. I don't know how to make it up to you."

Kerrie grinned and nodded. "Just don't tell Sam, okay?"

"Are you sure? I'll probably get fired, but maybe that's what I deserve."

"No, you don't. You love this stuff. You're going to be a great ranger some day. Look at your beard. It's nice and thick now. You even look like a ranger. Let's just keep this between us, okay?"

James nodded and reached down to hug Kerrie in an awkward motion. Kerrie stiffened slightly, but gave him a quick squeeze back. He walked past her toward the outhouse, and she stared after him, surprised that the embrace by the tall, young man hadn't sent her over the edge. She remembered the sight of Jack towering over her...a nightmare; the first time she'd met Dace in the bookstore, how tall he stood...how nervous and trapped she felt.

Kerrie squared her shoulders. Things had changed. *She* had changed. She entered the office with her head high.

Both Sam and Sandy were in the office, one working on the computer, the other counting money.

"Welcome back, kid," Sam swung around in his chair and regarded her. "How are you feeling?"

"Hey! You're back. I didn't think you'd come back." Sandy stood to give her a quick hug. "How are you?"

"I'm fine, fine." Kerrie knew she would be the center of attention for a while...about five minutes...and she'd already decided to grin and bear it.

"Uh...how was home? Your parents?"

"Good. Everyone was fine. It was nice to see them for a while. Thank you for the time off, Sam. It was great!"

"Good." He studied his nails for a moment before looking back up at her with a nod. "Good. Glad to hear it." He resumed his survey of his nails, palms, the back of his hands.

Kerrie regarded his behavior with suspicion, but was interrupted by Sandy.

"So, are you okay? Really?" She sat back down and gave Kerrie a pointed look, presumably leaving it up to Kerrie to interpret the question.

Kerrie realized they were shying away from direct mention of Jack. She took off her hat and sank into a chair.

"I'm okay. I think most of you know by now that I lived with a man in an abusive relationship for a long time and that I ran away and hid from him. He found me. Now, he's in jail, and I imagine he'll probably go to prison. It's over."

Sam abandoned his pretense and regarded her openly, his bald head nodding affirmatively.

"Yeah." The gruffness in his voice touched Kerrie.

"I'm sorry, Kerrie. I can't imagine..." Sandy allowed her words to trail off.

Kerrie cleared her throat and stood to put her hat on the shelf.

"So, who's next on the window?" she asked briskly.

Sam stood and pressed out the creases in his

trousers. "I think I'll head out there. You know, get some time in the trenches. Why don't you guys see about ordering a pizza for lunch? I'm buying."

Kerrie and Sandy stared after him in amazement as he grabbed a cash drawer and headed out the door.

"He's buying?" Sandy scrunched her face in disbelief.

"Lunch already?" Kerrie winced.

"Well, you're on the late shift. It's already eleven."

"So, it is."

"Hey, Kerrie, I've got some news."

A sense of foreboding settled on Kerrie, and she eyed Sandy's glowing cheeks with apprehension.

"Really?" Kerrie wasn't sure she could hear Sandy's voice over the mantra running through her head. *Please don't say anything I don't want to hear, please don't say anything I don't want to hear.*

Sandy beamed. "Yup. I-I'm getting married."

Kerrie watched in stunned silence as the elegant and sophisticated Sandy twirled around the room like a schoolgirl. She hardly seemed to notice Kerrie's frozen form.

"So, what do you think?"

Kerrie pushed herself forward in a fog of misery and embraced Sandy with cold hands.

"Congratulations, Sandy!"

Satisfied, Sandy twirled away again. "Isn't it great? I'm so happy. I'll send you an invitation, okay? We're going to do it soon. No point in waiting. I can't wait."

Kerrie sank into a chair and bit down hard to keep herself grounded in reality. "Soon?" she whispered.

"Yup, in the next couple of weeks. He's down at Yellowstone now, and I can't wait to get down there to see him. I miss him." Sandy pretended to pout, but her obvious joy ruined the effect. "Of course, I have to finish out my contract here next month, but after that, I'm heading down there."

"What wonderful news, Sandy." Kerrie clutched her stomach. "I'm thrilled to hear about it. Listen, I think I've got to head out to the outhouse. I'll be right back."

"Okay," Sandy sang, oblivious to Kerrie's distress. Kerrie brushed past James at the doorway and headed out across the parking lot. She bypassed the outhouse and headed into the woods following a well-worn deer trail as she broke into a run. She jumped over logs and ran through high grass until her sides truly ached. She stopped and bent over, hands on knees gasping. Tears rolled down her face and she brushed them away quickly. It wouldn't do to return to work with blurry eyes and a red nose. Allergy season had long since passed.

Kerrie straightened and tried to control her ragged breathing. Everything was going to be okay. Nothing had changed. Dace had always belonged to another. He'd never been hers.

She turned and retraced her steps slowly, wiping at her face. She wondered why Sandy and Dace decided to marry now, but imagined his departure for Yellowstone was a factor. It seemed clear that Sandy would follow him there. Kerrie brought her breathing under control, allowing clear thought to overtake her mild bout of hysteria.

Life would go on, it always did. Dace showed her what she wanted in a man, and she would wait until another man like him came along. If one ever did, she mused. In the meantime, she would return home this winter, perhaps to substitute teach, while she searched for another adventure next summer—another park in a similarly breathtaking location.

The following weeks passed in a blur of September visitors and the miracle of fall as the leaves of the trees burst out in a glorious array of oranges, reds, and yellows. Going to The Sun Road closed for the season and visitor usage dwindled accordingly.

Sandy took time off from work to prepare for her short-notice wedding at Yellowstone. Kerrie was grateful and avoided being alone with her to preclude any more confidences. She kept to herself for the most part, hoping for an end to the season...or at least an end to her misery in the form of Sandy's departure.

She visited the bookstore often and imagined Dace sitting across from her, teasing, challenging, blue-gray eyes tantalizing. She questioned her judgment in falling in love with first an abusive man...then an unavailable man. With a skeptical eye, she read self-help books on how to choose men, but tossed those aside for travel books and pictorials of national parks.

On occasion, Kerrie met the interested eyes of several men from across the room in the bookstore, but she looked away, no longer wondering if they stared at her. She didn't care. For now, she was still in love, and until that passed...with time and distance, she would entertain herself with books...not men.

Kerrie arrived home one night from her last week at work to find a white envelope in the mail. She stared at the return address. Sandy. The delicate square shape indicated an invitation...*the* invitation. Sandy mentioned she had put them in the mail the day before, hoping to wrap up all the details before her final day at work. Kerrie dropped it on a side table with no plans to open it. Unable to avoid staring at the elegant white square, she remembered an envelope her mother handed her in the hospital. Kerrie shook her head. In the rush to check out and leave the hospital, she'd forgotten about the business envelope. A twinge of guilt rushed through her. She hoped it wasn't a bill. Though insurance had taken care of most of the hospital payment, one never knew what hidden costs might appear. Kerrie turned and surveyed her apartment wondering where the envelope might be. She rifled through her papers but found nothing. She placed a call to her mother.

"Mom, do you remember giving me an envelope in the hospital? I don't remember who it was from. In fact, I'm not sure what it said."

"Well, hi, honey. How are you? Tomorrow is your last day at work, right?"

"Yes, I'll pack up after that and head back home. So, anyway, do you remember the envelope?"

"Yes. I gave it to you."

"But where did we put it?"

"Ummm...let me think. I put it in that little carryall we brought for you. In the side pocket, I think."

"Okay, Mom. Thanks. Talk to you soon."

"So, when are you coming home?"

"As soon as I've packed up and cleared the apartment. This weekend?"

"Okay, honey, see you then. Call me before you head out."

"Yes, Mom."

Kerrie closed the phone and headed for her closet to dig out the small blue travel bag her mother brought to the hospital. She rummaged in the side pocket and drew out the envelope. She remembered now. Her name was written across the front.

Concerned she had missed a bill, she opened the envelope. The bold handwriting indicated it was not a business correspondence, but personal.

Dear Kerrie,

It's late and you've fallen asleep again. I'm not sure, but I think they're giving you something to keep you sedated. I have to take off now, your family is here, but I wanted to leave a note for you in case I don't get to see you again before you leave for home. I'll probably be at Yellowstone before you return.

I'm not sure where we stand, Kerrie. I've tried to tell you how I feel, but you seem to stop me every time. In fact, you told me I had "no chance." But that's not what I read in your beautiful green eyes. I could be wrong. I hope I'm not wrong.

This is the worst possible time for me to tell you how I feel. You're in the hospital and you probably hate men right about now. I don't blame you. I'm afraid I might not get the chance to talk to you again. So, the note.

I love you. I think I fell in love with you the first time I saw you across the room at the bookstore. I love everything about you, the way you look, the way you walk, the way you laugh. I love your hair and your eyes and your mouth. I love your sense of humor and your vulnerability. I love your strength and your stubbornness. Well, I guess I just love you.

I don't know what your plans are for the future, but you know where I am. I'll call you when you get out of the hospital. I want you to come to Yellowstone with me. I want to spend the winter with you...and next summer...and the rest of my life. I know you're hesitant about leaving home, but I promise you we'll make a home wherever we are.

I love you, Kerrie. Please come to me.

Dace

Chapter Fourteen

Kerrie sank to the floor in stunned disbelief, her chaotic mind struggling to cope with a thousand scattered thoughts. He loved her. He was getting married. He loved her mouth. She never answered his phone calls. Kerrie drew her legs up and cringed. She never answered his phone calls. Maybe if she had. If he loved her, why would he marry someone else so soon? He loved her sense of humor. She wasn't sure she even had one anymore.

Kerrie laid the letter out on the floor and ran her fingers tenderly over the handsome writing. Bold like him.

Why was he marrying Sandy if he loved her?

For the life of her, she couldn't breathe and ran to the bathroom to splash cold water on her face. The water bit into her burning cheeks and she welcomed the sensation. Anything was better than the pain that ripped through her chest.

Kerrie returned to the bedroom and picked up the letter. She lay down on the bed and re-read the letter.

He loved her. And she had turned him away. Now he was marrying another. It seemed rushed, but...

With the intent to punish herself further, Kerrie got up and retrieved the wedding invitation with shaking hands. She lay back down on her bed and studied the envelope, holding it up to the light to see if she could read it without really having to see it. No luck.

A finger inserted under the edge and the envelope was open. She withdrew another envelope, the typical wedding invitation configuration, but unfortunately another hurdle for her to open.

She sat up and tossed the white square across the room. It landed on the floor by her dresser. What did it matter?

Kerrie grabbed her cell phone and studied it with desperate eyes. Her voice mail box was empty. She had deleted every one of Dace's messages without listening to them. Missed opportunities, missed chances.

Kerrie flopped onto her stomach with her head hanging off the end of her bed. The envelope lay on the floor only inches away from her eyes. She stared hard at it. He hadn't wasted any time proposing to Sandy it seemed. She needed a man with better staying power than that! After all, he'd been unfaithful to Sandy...perhaps not in deed, but there was no doubt he had flirted with Kerrie. And a proclamation of love to another woman was not the stuff of which loyal husbands were made.

With a full head of steam and an indignantly stiff backbone, Kerrie leaned over and grabbed the envelope. She opened it hurriedly and stared at the elegant engraved writing.

Sandra Darwood and William Sterling
request the honor of your presence
at their marriage on October twentieth of this year
at one p.m.
at the West Yellowstone Church of the Festivities.

Kerrie stared hard at the name on the invitation, her eyes playing tricks. *William Sterling. Bill Sterling. Billy Sterling. Sterling William.* Nothing remotely similar to *Dace Mitchell.* No possible combination could turn that name into *Dace Mitchell.*

She pressed the invitation close to her breast. The gurgling scream that emanated from her throat should have brought the neighbors running, but no one banged on the door. She jumped up from her bed, dancing, crying, laughing, and hooting, the invitation still clutched to her heart. Sandy was not marrying Dace. They had broken up...or something. Sandy was marrying William Sterling and Dace loved her... Or at least he had a month ago!

With shaking hands, Kerrie dialed the RSVP number on the invitation. The line rang and rang. Would Sandy answer? She needed to know what happened between her and Dace. Dare she ask?

"Hello?"

"Sandy?" Kerrie squeaked.

"Yes?"

"It's me, Kerrie. I got your invitation today." The

words spilled from her mouth like a flood. "It's beautiful. Congratulations. Really!"

"Oh, thank you, Kerrie. They are beautiful, aren't they? I had to rush to get them out. I'm so glad this was my last day at work. I'm packing up here to head out to Yellowstone to see Bill. How about you?"

"I didn't even know you were dating a Bill. I don't think you mentioned it." Kerrie's heart pounded in her ears.

"I know. I was being secretive. You know how it is when you first fall in love. You don't want to share it with anyone. Heck, I didn't even tell Dace."

Ahhh... The name she longed to hear. "Really?" she breathed. *Say more.*

"No, I didn't, and I tell him everything. Or I used to. I probably don't confide in him as much as I once did. I wasn't sure how he would feel about my dating another park ranger. Bill is a park ranger, you know."

"No, I didn't, although I thought I saw him one day."

"Yeah, dark hair and beard? That's him. What a doll."

How could she get Sandy to talk about Dace again? She took a deep breath.

"Well, congratulations again. How *is* Dace by the way?"

"He's fine, I guess. I don't know how well he likes it down there. He sounds kind of grumpy to tell you the truth. Kerrie..." Sandy hesitated. "Don't take this the wrong way, but I thought...I thought you guys were..."

Kerrie held her breath but Sandy stopped.

"What's that, Sandy?"

"I thought you guys were an item."

Kerrie pulled the phone away from her ear and stared at the mysterious creature for a moment.

"I-I don't know what you mean, Sandy. Oh, the hike and the assault and stuff!" She laughed nervously. "Oh, you know Dace. He thought I needed help. Nothing serious you know." Another hasty chuckle.

Sandy's voice deepened. "Gee, I don't know, Kerrie. I know my cousin pretty well. I think...I think he's in love with you. He doesn't talk to me about it, you know, but I've known him since we were kids, and he sure brightened up when you were around. Couldn't take his eyes off you."

"Your cousin?" Days, weeks, and months of unrequited love passed before Kerrie's eyes...wasted. "Your cousin?"

"Yeah. Dace."

Kerrie struggled for words. There were none. "I-I didn't know," she murmured with a breaking heart.

"Really? How could you not know? I thought everyone knew. Why do you think we're so close? You must have thought..." A mournful note crept into her voice. "Oh, Kerrie, did you think we were a couple?"

"I did," Kerrie whispered.

"Oh, geez, Kerrie. Wow, you must have thought he was quite the flirt. No wonder..."

Though she had little presence of mind left, Kerrie caught the odd note in Sandy's voice.

"What?"

"You're going to hate me for saying this. No wonder you seemed cold to him sometimes. I thought you two were a great match until I saw you ignore him a couple of times. Usually when I was standing around."

"Oh, dear, Sandy. That sounds horrible. Was I really that awful?"

"Not if you thought he was my guy." She chuckled. "Listen, he's at Yellowstone. I think you should call him. Tell him what you thought. Tell him you love him because I can hear it in your voice, Kerrie."

"I don't know, Sandy. It might be too late."

"It's never too late, my girl. Call him."

"I'll see if I can build up the courage."

"Good. I'll see you at the wedding."

Kerrie hung up without promising anything. If she couldn't face Dace, she most certainly could not show up at a wedding he would attend.

Chapter Fifteen

The blanket of white snow covering the valley brought the bison out in sharp relief. They buried their faces in the snow foraging for the grass buried beneath. Frost clung to their muzzles as they raised their heads to stare at her, a lone human in their midst. An occasional plume of white mist escaped the ground as the raging inferno deep beneath the earth's surface let off a little steam now and again. She dug her hands deeper into her pockets as she leaned against her truck. No other tourists or cars were in sight and she felt like she had the Park all to herself.

Yellowstone National Park in early winter shone just as bright as the colorful pictures in the books depicted it in the summer. When she left Columbia Falls yesterday, she'd driven straight down to southern Montana and spent the night in West Yellowstone.

Now, she didn't know what to do. Unwilling to face rejection over the phone, she hadn't called Dace as Sandy had commanded. But she wasn't looking forward to seeing his disappointment close up and in person either. After all, she'd ignored fourteen of his phone calls. That sort of behavior did little to help build a trusting relationship. She wouldn't blame him if he turned her away...if she even contacted him. What she should do is get back in her truck and return home to take time and sort things out.

Kerrie turned at the sound of an approaching vehicle. It had all the markings and appearance of a park ranger's SUV. A quiver passed through her body and her initial thought was to turn tail and run. Maybe it was William, Sandy's fiancée. Maybe there were lots of park rangers down here...even in the winter.

The SUV pulled up behind her, and Kerrie's body began to shake in earnest. Dace stepped out of the vehicle and moved toward her. He stopped for a second and stared at her, then opened his arms wide.

With a strangled cry of relief, Kerrie ran toward him and launched herself into his arms. His warm coat folded over her, and he enveloped her with strong, loving arms.

"I love you, Dace. I love you." She squeezed him with all her might.

"I love you, too, honey. I'm so glad to see you. I was going to give you one more week before I came to get you."

She couldn't hold back the tears that fell from her face. "I'm so sorry. I'm so sorry I didn't return your calls. I was so miserable."

She listened to the rumble of his chest against her ear as she pressed against him.

"I know, Kerrie. Sandy called. She doesn't keep secrets very well, that one. Well, at least anyone's but her own."

Kerrie peered up at his laughing face. She smiled. "I should have known she'd call you. I didn't know if you would still have me."

Dace lifted her chin so that she met his warm gaze. "I'd have you if a bear bit you and spit you back out." He grinned tenderly. "I'd have you if you never returned *any* of my calls." A slight wink. "I'd have you if you drank coffee instead of hot chocolate." He lowered his face toward hers, his lips tantalizingly close to her mouth. "I'd have you if you refused to marry me, but I hope you won't."

He pulled Kerrie to him, pressing his warm lips against her cold mouth, sending alternating shivers and hot thrills throughout her body all the way to her toes. She wrapped her arms around his torso and burrowed deeper into his coat. Dace backed up to lean against Kerrie's truck and pulled her tightly against his warm body as he explored her mouth. She stood on tiptoe, desperately trying to match the curves of her body with his, oblivious to public exposure, to the stares of the silent, watchful buffalo, to the cold frost on the trees above the road.

"Hey, sweetie." Dace straightened to look down into Kerrie's half-closed eyes. His ragged breathing came out in a cloud of frost. "I think we'd better take this somewhere private before I toss you down into a snow bank and have my way with you here."

Kerrie's eyes flew open, and she involuntarily stiffened. Dace caught the fleeting stillness.

"No, honey, not like that. I will never hurt you like that. You get to call the shots. You get to tell me what you want and don't want, okay?"

She lowered her face to his chest to listen for his heartbeat, to avoid the eyes that seemed to read her so well. Dace reached down with a gentle finger and lifted her chin.

"Okay?"

Kerrie stared into his warm gray eyes and nodded. "I'm sorry. I don't know how long this jumpiness will go on."

"It might go on for a long time, babe. It won't bother me. Not if I know you love me."

"I do love you, Dace...so much."

He grinned and pulled her tight. "Well, then, let's go home. I've got a surprise for you."

"Can you leave? Are you off duty?" Kerrie glanced up at him in surprise. What were the odds?

"I've been off for an hour. Believe it or not, I was just driving around..." His face took on a red tinge. Without looking at her, he reached for a lock of her hair and ran it between his fingers. "You're going to think I'm a lovesick fool. I was just driving around hoping I'd find you somewhere here...staring at the buffalo."

Kerrie threw back her head and laughed. "You know me well, don't you?" A curious buffalo turned in her direction. She lowered her voice to a whisper.

"Gosh, I hope he doesn't decide to come over."

"I doubt it. They're used to people." He kissed her cold nose and reluctantly let her go. "Come on, let's go."

Kerrie got into her car and followed Dace. His eyes, as he passed her to take the lead, spoke volumes. She became suddenly nervous. What was in store for her? All the fantasizing about him would soon come true. Could she handle being in such close proximity to a man...a tall man? Would her fears ruin everything? She kept her eyes on his SUV while she reassured herself. She had felt no fear when he held her in his arms. There was no reason to believe that her history with Jack would raise its ugly head once again and mar what promised to be a bright future.

She followed Dace to headquarters at Mammoth Hot Springs and waited for him to pick up his truck. While he checked in, she waited in the warm car and admired a herd of elk who lounged on the lawn in front of headquarters. They seemed to fear nothing and did not startle when Dace passed them to jump into his truck. By now, beginning to wonder where he lived, she followed him out of the Park through the north entrance. They traveled about twenty miles along a paved highway until Dace turned on a gravel road.

She followed him down the road and came to a stop behind him as he pulled up to a newer A-frame log cabin. He came to open her door with a surprisingly shy smile on his face.

"We're here."

"Is this where you live? It's great!" Kerrie turned to admire the lush spruce trees that surrounded the well-varnished pine cabin.

"Well, it's home for now. Come on in. The surprise is inside." He guided her with a hand to her back, an endearing gesture she had come to love.

She climbed sturdy wooden stairs and entered the cabin. Kerrie's nerves were taut. It seemed likely that he would make love to her, and she could think of nothing else. The comfortable pine furniture hardly caught her eyes as he pulled her coat from her shoulders.

"Do you want something hot to drink? Something to warm you up?" He stood behind her and bent his head to speak into her ear.

Kerrie held her breath, relishing the sound of his whisper against her ear. She shook her head. She would most likely choke on anything she tried to drink.

"Then let me show you my surprise." Dace shrugged out of his own coat and took her hand. He led her through the living room crowned by a cathedral ceiling and past a stone fireplace toward sliding glass doors which seemed to lead outside.

She hesitated for a moment, surprised by their destination. They were not heading for the bedroom as she anticipated...both with fear and excitement.

He pulled open the sliding glass doors and stepped

out onto a wooden deck. The sight of the snow-tossed valley which lay before them took her breath away. The stunning view of tree-lined ridges and rolling hills of white was magnificent.

Dace tugged her forward. "This is my surprise. When I saw this, I knew I had to take the cabin. I dreamed you'd be here with me."

Kerrie gasped as she looked at a hot tub set into the deck.

"It's fed by hot springs and it feels nice."

Kerrie turned to look at Dace and blushed at the look in his eyes.

"Now, Kerrie. It's time for us." He touched her cheek tenderly and leaned down to kiss her lips. "Tell me if you get scared." He murmured against her mouth as he pulled her to him. She shivered uncontrollably as he lowered a hand to the buttons of her blouse. His hand stilled. He raised his head and searched her face.

"Do you want me to stop?"

Kerrie shook her head vehemently. "Ignore any sounds or shivers. They won't be from fear." She surprised herself by pulling his head toward hers and wrapped herself around him.

Dace found the buttons and undid each one with exquisite deliberation, bending his head to allow his lips to follow his hands. Kerrie's knees weakened and she would have fallen had he not had his arms firmly wrapped behind her back.

Desperate to join with him, she unsnapped his shirt with one swift movement, eliciting a small strangled chuckle from him.

"Maybe I'm the one who needs to worry about you, tiger."

"Hurry up and get out of those clothes, ranger. I'm not sure how much longer I can wait."

He raised an eyebrow and grinned. "After you, ranger. I've been waiting for you a lot longer than you've been waiting for me."

Kerrie lowered her eyes and removed her slacks and underwear. She peeked over at Dace for just a moment to study the hard lines of his beautiful body as he dropped his clothes. The scars on his arm stood out vividly. She moved toward him and laid her face against the old wound.

"Bad bear," she whispered as she kissed the scar.

Dace gazed at her with a glint in his eye. In a swift movement, he picked Kerrie up in his arms and stepped into the steaming hot tub. He pulled her onto his lap and bent his head to her lips. She matched his kisses with a passion she had never known...ever.

Sometime later, Kerrie lay in his arms, sated and flush, his body protecting her from cold winds.

"I can't believe you read my mind."

"How's that, honey?" Dace murmured as he continued to kiss the back of her neck.

"That day, when we got back from Sperry Chalet, I didn't want you to leave me. All I wanted was for you to whisk me away to a spa and slip into a hot tub with me."

"And you have no idea how bad I didn't want to leave you."

She turned to nuzzle his neck. "It was a long summer," she murmured.

"The longest." He moved against her, passion rising once again.

"I love you, Dace."

"I love you too, Kerrie. I think I fell in love with you the first time I saw you across the room in the bookstore." His long, lingering kiss seemed to culminate an endless summer of desire on a trail of love. Kerrie knew she had the man of her dreams as she remembered her hopes that someday a gentle man would say to her: "I fell in love with you the first time I saw you across the room."

About the Author...

Bess McBride began her first fiction writing attempt when she was 14. She shut herself up in her bedroom one summer while obsessively working on a time travel/pirate novel set in the beloved Caribbean of her youth. Unfortunately, she wasn't able to hammer it out on a manual typewriter (oh yeah, she's that old) before it was time to go back to school. The draft of that novel has long since disappeared, but the story is still simmering within her, and she will get it written one day soon.

Bess was born in Aruba to American parents and lived in Venezuela until her family returned to the United States when she was 12. She couldn't fight the global travel bug within her and joined the U.S. Air Force at 18 to "see the world." After 21 wonderful and fulfilling years traveling the world and gaining one beautiful daughter, she pursued her dream of finally getting a college education. Armed and overeducated, the gypsy in her has taken over once again, and she is now embarking on a full-time journey in a recreational vehicle as she continues to look for new adventures and place settings for her writing. The Wild Rose Press has helped her fulfill a lifelong dream of writing romances.

Visit Bess' website at:

www.bessmcbride.com

Printed in the United States
206360BV00004B/139-159/P

9 781601 542991